This book belongs to:

....

....

....

Stories
for
8
Year Olds

Written by Moira Butterfield,
Jan and Tony Payne

Illustrated by Kate Sheppard
(Beehive Illustration)

Designed by Blue Sunflower Creative

This is a Parragon book
First published in 2005

Parragon
Queen Street House
4 Queen Street
BATH BA1 1HE, UK

ISBN 1-40544-724-9
Printed in England

Stories
for

8

Year Olds

p

Contents

Harold and the Missing Socks 7

The Tale of Two Witches 29

The Curse of Crumbly Castle 51

Stan's Sundae Secret 73

Top Secret 97

The Flying Pig 119

Get Me Out of Here! 141

The Most Dangerous Dragon 169

Harold
and the
Missing Socks

I 'll start by introducing myself. Harold is the name. Harold Hamster. I have pale brown fur and red eyes. I live in a cage in Michael Bogwell's bedroom and I like carrots, taking naps and shredding paper.

Michael is my owner. He's nearly nine years old. He likes football, crisps and watching TV. Luckily, I like all three of these too, so we get along fine. His room is usually a peaceful place except when his mum comes in to clean it up.

Michael's mum is called Cheryl. She likes magazines, aerobics and shoes. What she doesn't like is the mess that Michael makes. I have to say, Michael is a bit of a slob, so his mum does have a point. Unfortunately she makes the point by shouting obvious things, such as: "You've thrown your crisp packets on the floor!" and "This place is like a pigsty," etcetera, etcetera. When she shouts like that she gives me a headache.

Michael lets me watch football on TV with him, and feeds me crisps, so I reckon I owe him a lot, which is why I took on the Case of the Missing Socks.

I first realized there were mysterious happenings in the Bogwell household when Michael was rummaging in his room one morning. He was holding one of his favourite spotty socks in his hand. He called,

"Mum, I can't find my other sock." His mum came in to his bedroom to help him look. But she couldn't find the matching sock either.

"I don't know where all the missing socks go. I put them in the wash and half of them disappear," sighed Cheryl the Mum.

Michael's sister, Kylie, walked by at that moment (she likes biscuits, music and mobile phones).

"Has anyone seen my other stripy sock?" she asked accusingly.

Just then, Michael's dad appeared at the door. His name is Dave. He likes sport, toffee and going to the garden shed.

"One of my golf socks is missing too," he remarked. "Maybe there's a sock monster in the washing machine that gobbles up one sock from every pair! Or maybe one of the pets is eating them!"

Clearly, he is mad. But for a moment I thought I saw Michael's mum looking suspiciously at me. She couldn't think I was stealing the family socks, could she? Would she take revenge on me and cut down my carrot supply? If I was wrongly accused, it could be very serious. What would happen then? I could be abandoned on the street without even a cage to my name!

Looking back, perhaps I was worrying too much. But at the time I felt I had to act.

At this point, Royston, the family dog, enters my story. He's a bit hairy and drools sometimes, but he's nice enough to me. He likes food, chewing things and barking when the doorbell goes.

"Royston, I need a word with you... confidentially," I whispered to him.

"Confi-what-ally?" he replied. I had forgotten for a brief moment how awesomely thick he is.

"Confidentially means 'in secret'," I explained. "Listen carefully. There is a crisis and we are under suspicion. A number of socks have gone missing. We need to find them, or our cosy lives here could be over!"

Royston looked even more confused than normal.

"Socks, Royston. Socks!" I tried to make it simple for him to understand. "Some of them have disappeared and we are the prime suspects. We have to find them before we are thrown out onto the street!"

Royston grinned lopsidedly. I sighed and, for a moment, I wished that the Bogwells had chosen a cleverer pet – a parrot or a gerbil, perhaps – to keep me company. Frankly, a stick insect would probably have more brainpower than dear old Royston. Still, I was stuck with him so I had to make the best of it.

Of course, I couldn't do the sock-hunting myself because a) I couldn't get out of my cage easily and b) it would be very dangerous for me to roam around the house. Dave the Dad might fail to see me and step on me with one of his unbelievably large trainers. Or Cheryl the Mum might spear me to the carpet with her high heels. No. Royston would have to do the searching, so I briefed him on my list of possible sock hideaways.

"Look for Michael's missing spotty sock," I advised him. "If we find that, my guess is we'll solve the mystery."

I swiftly worked out a list of places for Royston to search for the socks:

1. The washing basket.
2. Michael's bedroom floor.
3. The cupboard in the bathroom.
4. Underneath the sofa cushions.

It seemed simple, but it turned out to be a disaster due to the breathtaking stupidity of Royston. He tipped up the washing basket and scattered the clothes all over the floor. He snuffled around Michael's bedroom and accidentally knocked over a can of very sticky fizzy drink. He managed to drool all over Kylie's clean T-shirt in the airing cupboard. By the time he had finished searching under the cushions it looked as if a hurricane had struck.

Royston was in disgrace. He was shut in the kitchen for the rest of the day and could no longer help out with the sock search. I had to try something else fast. If socks were missing, somebody might be stealing them. I worked out a list of suspects in my mind.

Michael – surely he wouldn't steal his own socks unless he had gone completely mad?

Cheryl the Mum – she would also need to be mad to steal the socks. She is slightly crazy, come to think of it.

Kylie the Sister – very unlikely. She often says that Michael's socks are 'disgusting' and would not go near them.

Dave the Dad – clearly mad. His suggestion of the sock monster could be a clue. A definite possible sock-stealer.

I had to come up with a plan. But all this thinking and worrying about being made homeless was giving me a headache. So I went for a lie-down.

The next day a vital new piece of

evidence came my way. Cheryl the Mum came in and started talking about the missing socks again:

"I can't understand it. Dave, do you think they're in the back of the washing machine?"

Then Dave the Dad put his head around the bedroom door.

"Don't keep going on about the missing socks," he cried. "I've had the missing socks up to here." He gestured to the top of his head.

So he admitted it! He'd 'had the missing socks', which meant he'd stolen them, a great pile reaching up to his head! Nobody else seemed to notice what he'd said, probably because nobody listened to him. But I had heard! I knew he was guilty! Now all I had to do was prove it.

Royston had been forgiven for his bad behaviour and was roaming around the house again. I was able to ask him a few questions about Dave the Dad's behaviour.

"Where are his favourite places in the house? One of these could be his sock hiding place," I said. Once Royston had stopped scratching his ear, he was able to give me the following list of Dave the Dad's favourite places:

1. The armchair.
2. The garage.
3. The shed.

I realized that this time I would have to do the searching myself. I couldn't ask Royston again. He'd got into trouble last time and he was rubbish at sock-hunting anyway. I would have to risk my life to save the Bogwells.

"Open my cage, Royston," I commanded. He used his ridiculous long nose to move the hook that kept my cage door secure, and I climbed out. I jumped onto his back and held on tight.

"Take me to Dave the Dad's favourite armchair," I declared. I had a white-knuckle ride on Royston's back as he lolloped downstairs. By the time we got to the sitting room I was feeling quite travel-sick.

I slipped off my dog taxi onto the armchair and began to burrow down the side of the seat cushion. Here I found a wide range of surprising objects, which I took to be a selection of Dave the Dad's other stolen treasures. There were coins and a plastic toy from a cereal packet. He must have stolen it from his own children! There was also a golf tee, several balls of fluff (which I suppose he stole for insane reasons of his own) and a toffee he was no doubt saving for a special occasion. What a villain!

I gnawed a hole in the chair lining and

burrowed down further. Underneath I found a barren world of dead beetles and grit. No socks, though. I came up sneezing, my fur covered in dust.

"He's clever, I'll give him that. Evil but clever," I remarked to a bemused Royston. "He probably thought the armchair was too obvious a hiding place for his sock hoard. Royston, take me to the garage."

Once more I held on to Royston's unpleasantly smelly fur, keeping my eyes tightly shut as he trotted through the kitchen, pushed open a side door and then stepped into the garage. I'd never seen this mysterious place before, but I could tell it was the den of a madman. It was dark and shadowy, with shelves crammed with half-open tins, rusty tools and paintbrushes that had gone hard. Only someone crazy would have tried to use these things. I thought I smelt the faint odour of mice out here. Perhaps they had a nest amongst the chaos. They never showed themselves, but I had the feeling they might be watching me. I didn't think mice would harm me, but you never know. Mice living in Dave the Dad's den might be odd.

I began to search the garage for socks. It was very hard work for me. I nosed in every corner, round every box and under every old tyre. Finally I climbed beneath the car, which was pretty scary. By the end I felt tired and greasy, but was no nearer to discovering the truth. There were no socks in the garage. It was time for my biggest challenge.

"He's hidden them in the shed," I

breathed. Royston took me back to the kitchen, but we found the back door to the garden shut. I hopped up onto the windowsill. If I wanted to get to the shed I would have to squeeze through the open window and make the journey myself.

The garden looked enormous, stretching away into the distance. At the far end the shed stood dark and brooding. I was sure the missing socks were there, hidden away by the madman Dave the Dad. But out there it would be as dangerous for me as an African safari. Unknown hazards, wild creatures and vile insects might lay in wait. I began to feel cowardly. Why bother? Perhaps the Bogwells would forget about the missing socks. Perhaps I needn't risk my life.

As I wavered, Cheryl the Mum came stomping into the kitchen. I dived behind a convenient flowerpot and listened to her muttering as she loaded the washing machine with more laundry.

"I don't suppose I'll see half these socks again. And who's going to do anything about it? Nobody but me, that's who..."

That made up my mind for me. Unless this mystery was solved for good we pets would soon suffer. I swallowed hard and slipped through the open window into the dreaded garden.

At first I scampered thoughtlessly up the path, trying to get to the shed as fast as I could. But then I realized I was in full view of any birds who might fancy carrying me away to their nest for a mid-morning snack. I had to act more cleverly, more like a special agent. I dived into a small clump of leaves and blundered into a spider's web that stuck unpleasantly over my face.

"Hey! Look what you've done, furball!" the angry spider shouted at me.

"Sorry. Got to go," I cried and ran on, zig-zagging between bushes and flowers. I daren't look up in case I saw the shadow of some vicious bird, so I kept my eyes on the shed. I ran for my life, and I'm proud to say I made it.

Getting into the shed was simple as it was as ramshackle and badly repaired as most of the other things that belonged to Dave the Dad. I just skirted around the outside until I found a loose plank for me to slip through.

Inside there was a musty smell coming from open bags of compost. There were piles of crusty flowerpots and rusty tools. The place was an animal graveyard. Dead flies lay trapped in spiders' webs. A dead moth was caught in a roll of fence wire. A dead bumble bee lay drying out on the windowsill. I'm sure I smelt something decaying under the flowerpots, but couldn't bear to look. I stared around wildly for the pile of stolen socks, and my heart began to sink. They weren't there.

How could I have been so wrong? My mind was racing. I slipped back into the garden, desperate to get back to the house and into my cage so I could think clearly. But I didn't get far before a soft voice hissed in my ear.

"Oh good. Here's dinner," it said chillingly. I was bowled over by a paw, and as I tumbled to the ground I saw the vicious face of Tiddles the Cat from next door. I'd forgotten about Tiddles, and now I was going to pay with my life! I had never met her but I knew all about her from Royston, her arch-enemy. His personal goal in life was to chase her forever from the Bogwell garden. I felt faint with fear.

"Just kill me," I cried.

"My pleasure," Tiddles grinned and scooped me up in her mouth.

But just then her ears went flat, her hair stood on end and she whipped around. Royston was bounding up the path, barking loudly. Someone had let him out at just the right moment.

Tiddles jumped onto the garden fence. In her hurry to get away, she hurled me high into the air. I flew helplessly up and then began to plunge down towards the earth, and my certain death, or so I thought. In fact I didn't quite reach the ground. Instead I fell into a duvet cover hanging on the Bogwell's washing line. I tumbled to the bottom and fell onto a soft pile of socks.

What luck! At last I had found the missing hoard! I realized they had been caught inside the duvet cover while tumbling around in the washing machine. I had accused poor Dave the Dad but he was an innocent man. How stupid I had been. Nobody had stolen the Bogwells' socks, and I could rest easy.

I fell into a deep calming sleep and when I woke I crawled out of the duvet cover and found I was now in the washing basket in the kitchen. I carefully hauled out each missing sock and laid them, one by one, on top of the laundry for Cheryl the Mum to see.

The only odd thing was the absence of Michael's favourite spotty sock. It wasn't with the others.

"Perhaps it got caught up in a sleeve or a pillowcase," I thought, but I learned the truth when I glanced out of the window.

Royston was sitting on the lawn and I realized he was chewing Michael's spotty sock! I watched him, appalled, as he then trotted over to a flowerbed and buried the sock in the soft earth. Royston was a sock-stealer, not a serious one, but guilty nevertheless. I confronted him with the evidence when I was safely back in my cage.

"Oh, so that's a sock," he said. "I didn't know what you were talking about before but I didn't like to ask. I thought you were just bonkers." He smiled stupidly. Me bonkers? The idiot hound hadn't even known what socks were. He'd just played along with me.

"But why did you steal the spotty one?" I asked.

"I wanted it because it's cuddly. Will I have to give it back?" he replied, looking worried.

There was nothing more to say. I had found where the guilt lay. No harm was done really, and the Bogwell family survived the whole sorry episode. Michael got new socks and Royston promised he wouldn't borrow them. I had to forgive him. After all, he had saved my life.

"Thank goodness hamsters don't wear socks," I thought to myself when it was all over, and when I later heard Kylie complaining about all her missing pairs of knickers...well, I pretended not to hear.

The Tale of Two Witches

It was the start of a new term at the Witch Academy and Clara and Chloe were late. Clara and Chloe still didn't know very much. They were going to school to learn how to be good witches.

"Hurry up, Clara," said Chloe.

"I am hurrying up," replied Clara. She still wasn't dressed, and Chloe was becoming rather impatient. She always seemed to be waiting for Clara these days.

"I won't be long, I promise," said Clara.

"Use the 'Get dressed quickly' spell," said Chloe.

"OK," said Clara. "I think I can remember the words." She began to chant loudly:

"Tara-diddle, tara-di,
Socks and knickers come to me.
Hurry, clothes, come straight away –
I've got to go to school today!"

Then she pointed a finger at her clothes. But instead of coming to dress Clara, the clothes flew out of the window and dressed Billy Brewster next door! He was really surprised. He'd never worn a girl's dress before.

Chloe and Clara looked out of the window and giggled.

"How did that happen?" asked Clara.

Things like this were always happening to Clara. She read her spell book. She did her homework. She tried really hard, but her spells always seemed to go wrong.

"I'll get them back," said Chloe. She went to the window and pointed her finger at Billy Brewster:

"Tara-diddle, tara-di,
Socks and knickers come to me.
Hurry, clothes, come straight away –
So we can go to school today!"

The clothes flew off Billy Brewster and landed in a heap on Clara. They quickly sorted themselves out and got her dressed. The shoes went on last. The laces quickly tied themselves and then the two little witches grabbed some breakfast and hurried off to school.

Wizard Warlock was waiting for them when they arrived.

"You're late," he said, looking at his watch. Wizard Warlock was the headmaster. In fact he was head of everything. He taught lessons. He taught games and he taught magic. He even made the school dinners.

Of course, he had lots of spells and potions to help him. He had a spell for

cooking and he had a spell for washing up afterwards. He had a spell for marking books and a spell for teaching sums.

This morning he was getting to know everyone. On the desk in front of him sat Malice, his black cat. Malice didn't like girls. He wished that Wizard Warlock would turn them all into white mice.

Malice did like white mice!

Wizard Warlock called out the girls' names.

"Serena?"

"Here, Wizard Warlock."

"Maddy?"

"Here, Wizard Warlock."

"Marie-Claire?"

"Ici, Monsieur Wizard Warlock." Marie-Claire was French and very polite.

"Chloe, Clara?"

"Here, Wizard Warlock," said Chloe and Clara. They were still panting from running all the way to school. They couldn't wait until they were old enough to ride a broomstick. They wouldn't be late then. Wizard Warlock wrote everyone's name in a big black book. When he had finished he closed it with a snap.

"Today," he said, "we are going to have a spelling test. Use this spell to help you – 'Hocus pocus, help me focus'. Got that?"

The little witches nodded and picked up their pens.

"The first word is 'caterpillar'."

The witches looked at each other. It was a hard word but they had the spell to help them.

"Hocus pocus, help me focus," they chanted, and began writing. When they finished they showed Wizard Warlock.

Chloe, Maddy and Serena had spelled it correctly. Vesta and Venetia had got one letter wrong. Marie-Claire had written it in French. And Clara had written... 'Pottydrawers'.

"Pottydrawers!" said Wizard Warlock, raising his bushy eyebrows. "What are pottydrawers?"

"I don't know," said Clara. "Are they drawers that have gone potty?" Everyone giggled.

"Quiet please," said the wizard. "Let's all try an easier word. 'Tomatoes'."

Clara picked up her pen, then chanted

the spell slowly and clearly.

"Hocus pocus, help me focus." She pressed the pen to the paper.

'Tantrums' wrote the pen, then made a black blob of ink.

"Oh!" said Clara.

Wizard Warlock didn't say anything, but his eyebrows shot up until they disappeared under his pointed hat.

"I got the 'T' right," said Clara.

On the way home from school Chloe and Clara stopped to get a milkshake at the local café.

"I'll never get the hang of this magic thing," said Clara, sipping her banana milkshake.

"You will," said Chloe. "Practice, that's all it takes. See that boy over there, he's dripped tomato ketchup on his school tie. Use some magic to get it off."

"OK. I'll give it a go," said Clara.

Clara took a deep breath, pointed her finger at the tie and began to repeat the spell:

> *"Sticky stains are*
> *pretty manky.*
> *Wipe them with*
> *a magic hanky."*

The sisters waited for a moment, then Clara nudged Chloe. "Look!" she whispered. "It worked. The stain's disappeared." Chloe looked.

"So has most of the tie," she whispered back. "Now he's got a big hole in it."

"Whoops," said Clara, "Quick, do something before he notices."

Chloe hesistated a moment, then she slowly pointed her finger and muttered:

"See the hole
in that boy's tie?
Mend it quickly –
don't ask why!"

In a flash the tie was back to normal.

"Phew!" breathed Clara. "That was close."

"Try something else," said Chloe.

Clara looked around. A waitress was trying to carry a tray full of dirty dishes.

"That looks like hard work," said Clara. "I'll make the tray as light as a feather."

Clara scrunched up her face and concentrated hard. Then she pointed at the tray. Chloe could see her lips moving.

There was a loud crash as the tray toppled sideways and the dishes fell to the floor. All the customers looked around and the manager came rushing out through a swing door.

"What's going on?" he asked.

Before the waitress had time to explain Chloe had put things right. The dishes were back, and the tray was balanced lightly on the waitress's hand.

"Nothing, Mr Phipps," she said, almost dancing through the swing doors into the kitchen.

When Chloe and Clara got back home they started to tidy the house.

"You do upstairs," said Chloe, "and I'll do downstairs."

Clara started with her bedroom. It was in a mess. The bed wasn't made and the cupboard door had burst open. Toys were spilling out all over the place. She couldn't see her desk for screwed-up paper, and her clothes were in a heap on the floor.

"Where shall I start?" thought Clara. "This is going to take forever. I'll use a spell to speed things up."

She read the 'Tidy' spell in her book. Pointing her finger at the clothes, she repeated:

> *"Diddly do-da,*
> *diddly squat,*
> *Mess and muddle,*
> *clear the lot."*

Then she pointed at the paper on the desk and the toys falling out of cupboard. "That should do it," she said to herself.

Downstairs, Chloe was coming out of the kitchen when she heard a roar coming from Clara's room. Just in time she flattened herself against the wall as all Clara's belongings hurtled down the stairs.

"Don't stop me!" yelled Crazy Clown, racing past.

"Get out of our way!" shouted a family of pink hippos.

"I'm free, I'm free!" laughed a huge bouncy ball.

Chloe stayed flat against the wall as clothes, toys, books and computer games flew past. Even Clara's bed tried to escape, but ended up wedged near the door next to the hatstand.

"Stop," called Chloe after them. "Stop at once!"

She pointed a finger at the chaos in the hallway. Then she began to speak in a loud voice:

"Clothes and books and bouncy ball,
Everything that's in the hall.
Stop this nonsense right away,
Be neat and tidy from today."

The toys, the games and the clothes slowly came to a halt.

Then, grumbling a bit, they turned around and went back to Clara's bedroom. The toys piled into the cupboard, and the door shut with a bang. The clothes folded themselves up and disappeared into drawers. The desk tidied itself and put all the screwed-up paper into the waste basket. The books got back onto the bookshelf. The bed heaved itself into position. And the bouncy ball bounced back up the stairs, sat in a corner and sulked.

Chloe and Clara sat at the kitchen table and shared a packet of crunchy peanut crackers. "I think we've got a problem," said Chloe.

"So do I," agreed Clara.

The next day at the Witch Academy the two little witches told Wizard Warlock what had happened.

He listened carefully. When he heard the bit about the talking toys he couldn't help smiling. He gave Malice the cat a pat on the head.

"Don't worry," he said kindly. "We'll get to the bottom of this, you'll see."

But over the next few days, Clara accidentally turned a lady's hat into a bunch of bananas. She gave herself a mermaid's tail instead of a new pair of shoes. And she filled the local swimming pool full of frogspawn. Chloe was rushed off her feet putting everything back to normal again.

It was almost the day of the school's summer fair.

"I want everyone to organize a stall at the school fair this year," said Wizard Warlock.

"Let's have a candyfloss stall," said Serena.

"And a roundabout," said Maddy.

"A hall of mirrors," said Marie-Claire.

"What about a coconut shy?" said Chloe.

"A ghost train!" said Clara. They were all very excited.

All the little witches got magic spells ready. Wizard Warlock watched carefully so they didn't make any mistakes. But Clara was still having trouble with her spell.

"I'll help you," smiled Wizard Warlock. He was determined to find out what Clara was doing wrong to cause so much havoc.

The sun was shining on the morning of the school fair. The whole class arrived at school very early to put up the stalls and rides.

"I'll start first," said Wizard Warlock, and quick as a flash he conjured up a helter-skelter.

Next, Serena said her spell and a candyfloss stall appeared. Maddy conjured up a magic roundabout and Marie-Claire produced a hall of magic mirrors with a flourish.

"Now you, Chloe," said Wizard Warlock.

Chloe said her spell loudly and clearly. Then she pointed her finger and a stall with the words 'Coconut Shy' appeared, with coconuts balanced on top of poles, colourful plastic balls to throw at the coconuts and lots of prizes.

Wizard Warlock turned to Clara. "Your turn, Clara," he said. "You do the ghost train."

Slowly and clearly Clara chanted the spell:

"Phantoms, ghouls and
spooky ghosts,
Scare me with your moans and wails.
Give me goosebumps big as eggs,
Or I'll turn you into snails."

Then she looked at Wizard Warlock. He nodded. Clara took a deep breath and pointed her finger.

There was a flash of lightning, followed by an enormous crack of thunder. Then it started to rain. Huge drops hit the ground and bounced up again. Malice the cat jumped into Clara's arms, his fur standing up straight in fright.

"Try the spell again," yelled Wizard Warlock over the noise of the crashing thunder. It wasn't easy with Malice tucked in her right arm, but Clara did as she was told. She repeated:

*"Phantoms, ghouls and
spooky ghosts,
Scare me with your moans and wails.
Give me goosebumps big as eggs,
Or I'll turn you into snails."*

And this time she pointed with the first finger of her left hand.

Straight away, the thunder and lightning stopped. The rain cleared away and the wind died down. As the sun came out, they could see a building that hadn't been there before. It had **GHOST TRAIN** in orange and red letters on the front. There was a tunnel at the entrance and a train was going in. They could hear loud moans and wails as the ghosts began to practise.

Clara clapped her hands. "I did it," she laughed. "I did it!" Chloe hugged her.

"Clara, are you left-handed?" asked Wizard Warlock.

"I guess I am!" said Clara in surprise.

"So that was the problem," said Wizard Warlock, looking as pleased as punch. "You were using your right hand – but you're left-handed!"

"Can I do something else?" asked Clara. She didn't want to stop now. "Can I make the big dipper?"

"Why not?" said Wizard Warlock.

Laughing out loud, Clara called out her spell loud and clear, being sure to point her left finger this time:

"Snails and lizards, toads and frogs,
Slimy slugs and squelchy bogs.
Mix some magic in a pot,
Stir a little, not a lot.
Say 'Whipper Snapper,
Snapper Whipper',
And send me now a huge big dipper!"

There was a whirl of wind. Then, as suddenly as it had come, the wind died away. Towering above them the wizard and

the two little witches could see the twinkling fairy lights of the biggest big dipper they had ever seen.

"Brilliant," shouted Clara.

"Amazing," shouted Chloe.

"Fantastic," shouted Wizard Warlock.

"No way!" mumbled Malice the cat.

The fair was a huge success. Children came from miles around to enjoy it. And, as a reward for all their hard work, Wizard

Warlock took all the little witches from the Witch Academy on the rides free.

There was only one mishap. When Clara was in the haunted house, she accidentally waved her right hand and turned one of the ghosts into a giant coconut. Unfortunately she forgot to turn him back, so if you should ever visit a fair and go on a ghost train, and hear a giant coconut moaning and wailing, try not to laugh. He is only doing his best to be really scary.

The Curse
of
Crumbly
Castle

Sssh!

Daisy was only a small princess, but she was good at telling big tall tales, as you will see. She lived in Crumbly Castle, home of the noble and ancient Crumbly family for hundreds of years. It had lots of spiky-shaped towers and turrets, so old and cracked they had begun to lean this way and that like a set of rotten wiggly teeth.

One night Daisy was busy playing. (Princesses in Crumbly Castle are allowed to play at night.) She ran in and out of 100 secret spidery rooms, then marched up and down in the giant kitchen, pretending to be an army general. She was just about to shout out "Halt!" to her imaginary soldiers when she heard a creaking noise behind her, and the kitchen window swung open on its rusty hinges. Daisy hid inside one of the big kitchen cupboards and crouched there, peeping out through a tiny gap between the saucepans.

From her hiding place she saw two burglars climbing in through the window. One was short, round and very hairy, with eyebrows that joined in the middle and looked like a black caterpillar sitting on his forehead. The other was long and thin and had no hair on his head at all. Bristly tufts came out of his ears and nose instead.

Once these two were in, they pulled a big empty sack in behind them and began to tiptoe softly across the kitchen floor.

"BOO!" Daisy cried, and she jumped out of her hiding place as pots and pans clattered onto the floor around her. The burglars squealed and leapt onto the kitchen table, thinking at first that she was a fierce guard dog. They shook like bowls of jelly until they realized that she was only a small girl.

"You'd better stay quiet," growled the hairy burglar. "Otherwise we'll put you in our sack along with all the stuff we're going to steal!" He climbed off the table and scowled nastily, wiggling his eyebrow caterpillar to scare Daisy. This didn't work because Daisy wasn't scared of anything.

"There's no need to be so rude," she replied. "I don't care whether you steal every last little thing. I won't tell. In fact, I know this castle from top to bottom. I can show you where the best treasures are, if you like."

The burglars thought about it, which didn't take long because they were very stupid.

"OK," they agreed. "But don't try any

funny business, all
right?"

"Certainly not!"
Daisy shook her head,
looking shocked at the
very idea.

So that's how
Daisy ended up
taking two burglars
on a tour of her
home, pointing out
all the best treasures
for stealing.

Or so they thought...

First she took them to the Great
Dining Room, where all the castle's famous
silver cutlery was laid out in gleaming rows.
There were shiny silver knives, forks,
spoons and lots of other bits of cutlery that
nobody could quite remember what to do
with.

"Wow! Let's put this lot in our sack!" the burglars declared excitedly.

"I wouldn't do that if I were you," Daisy replied. "You see, there's a terrible curse on anyone who takes this cutlery."

"You what?" the hairy burglar stared at her.

"How can there be a curse on knives and forks?" the bald burglar added disbelievingly.

"I'll tell you a true story that proves it," Daisy replied in a serious voice. "Many years ago the Tenth Lord Crumbly held a grand Christmas dinner here for all his relatives. It went very well until his greedy Great Aunt Maud stole a silver teaspoon. 'It's just a silly little spoon,' thought Great Aunt Maud. 'But it's rather pretty. I'd like it for my sugar bowl at home. No one will miss it.' She hid the spoon under her skirt and left with it at the end of the party. But she got no further than the front door."

"Why? What happened?" the bald burglar demanded.

"A giant eagle swooped down and carried her off," Daisy whispered, as if she was telling them a terrible secret. "I know it's hard to believe, but it was all caused by the cutlery curse, you see. The eagle carried Aunt Maud for thousands of miles and then dropped her in the middle of a steamy smelly jungle. She was captured by a local tribe and forced to mend their steamy smelly socks for 20 years."

"People who live in the jungle don't wear socks," the hairy burglar pointed out suspiciously.

"Normally they wouldn't, but remember that Great Aunt Maud was cursed, so unluckily for her the tribe that caught her wore two pairs each," Daisy explained, quick as a flash.

"Are you making this up?" the hairy burglar growled, looking closely at Daisy's face. She looked completely innocent.

"We don't want to take the chance, Cyril. We'd better leave the cutlery behind," the bald burglar muttered worriedly.

Then Daisy took out a fluffy sticky old sweet from her pocket and popped it on the table when the burglars weren't looking.

"Take this precious ruby instead," she suggested, pointing to the sweet. "It's the Royal Sticky Ruby of Timbuctoo. It brings all its owners good luck."

"That's more like it," the stupid burglars grinned and dropped the sweet into their sack.

Next, Daisy led them through the dark and echoing Great Entrance Hall.

"Shall we nick this?" the hairy burglar suggested, pointing to an ugly but very rare and valuable vase at the bottom of the stairs.

"Mmm, you could do that," Daisy put her finger to her lips thoughtfully. "But it's not a good idea, what with the curse and everything. If you damaged it, you'd be in big trouble, believe me."

"How do you know there's a curse on this?" the burglars gasped.

"Because there's a famous story that proves it," Daisy declared. "One day the Eighth Lord Crumbly's butler slid down the stair banisters for a laugh. He came down on the seat of his shiny butler's trousers and he got faster and faster until he flew off the end of the stairs like a rocket. He crashed into the vase, chipping it badly. He was just dusting himself down when the front door burst open and a gang of fearsome pirates swarmed in."

"Due to the curse?" the bald burglar asked.

"Of course," Daisy nodded. "They dangled from the chandeliers and swung on the curtains, and when they got bored doing that they carried the butler off to their ship and sailed around the world. They made him peel potatoes for weeks, but he got away in the end..."

"Had the curse worn off?" the bald burglar asked hopefully.

"Not exactly," Daisy muttered. "The pirate ship sank in a storm but the butler was rescued..."

"That's all right then," the hairy burglar grinned and reached for the vase.

"...by a ship called *The Titanic,* the

famous one that got hit by an iceberg," Daisy added.

The burglar snatched his hand away from the vase.

While they weren't looking, Daisy pulled out some old fishbones she had found in the kitchen. She put them down near the vase, then pointed them out.

"You must take this," she insisted. "It's a set of dinosaur bones so it's worth a lot of money."

"It looks like a fish to me," the hairy burglar frowned.

"The very first fish ever," Daisy added quickly.

"Crumbs!" the hairy burglar grinned and popped the bones into the sack.

Next Daisy took them to the Castle Art Gallery, where there were rows and rows of portraits showing pretty people, ugly people and one or two utterly hideous people from the past, all of them members of the Crumbly family. The biggest, best and most valuable masterpiece was at the very end of the row. It showed the 14th Lord Crumbly painted by a famous modern artist, with his nose upside down and his head underneath his knee.

"Now that *is* worth stealing, don't you think, Ernie?" the hairy burglar gasped, and he pushed the bald burglar towards it.

"I don't think so," Daisy shook her head, sucking air in between her teeth.

"Another curse?" the bald burglar sighed despairingly.

"How did you guess?" Daisy smiled ruefully. "I'd better tell you the story before you do something you'll regret. Some years ago the Earl of Moneypile was a guest of the 14th Lord Crumbly. The Earl won that painting from Lord Crumbly by cheating at 'Snap'. He carried it out to his car but he didn't get much further..."

"What was it this time? Pirates or giant eagles?" the hairy burglar asked.

"Neither. He was attacked by unbelievably large mice," Daisy whispered, making her eyes go round with shock.

"I would never have guessed that!" the hairy burglar cried, and his eyebrow caterpillar shot up in surprise.

"A whole herd of them appeared from nowhere and galloped right over the Earl," Daisy continued.

"Did he die?" the bald burglar asked, stepping back nervously from the painting.

"No, he didn't die," Daisy explained. "He was completely flattened, though, just like a piece of paper or a pancake. He stayed that way for the rest of his life. He was so flat he could slip under doors without having to open them, but apart from that it was very inconvenient."

"Forget the painting, Cyril," the bald burglar muttered and his terrified hairy friend nodded in agreement.

"This is the treasure you should take," Daisy said, pointing to a garbage bin full of screwed-up sweet wrappers, mouldy sandwiches and used lolly sticks left by gallery visitors the day before.

"This is a modern sculpture by somebody very well known. Of course, you knew that, I'm sure," Daisy looked sideways at the amazed burglars.

"Oh, er, yes. We recognized it straight away," the hairy burglar lied and quickly stuffed the bin into the sack.

Next Daisy led the burglars to the Grand Armoury, where knights' helmets, swords and suits of armour were displayed. The burglars rushed up to the biggest, shiniest suit.

"We'll take this one," they cried. "It's the biggest so it must be the best!"

"It's also the oldest," Daisy remarked. "Beware. Old curses are the worst."

"Oh no," the bald burglar cried, holding his head in his hands. The hairy one thumped the wall angrily, and then looked scared when the suit of armour wobbled. Daisy let out an exaggerated gasp so they knew she was about to tell another horrible story.

"Take care!" she cried, and then made her voice go soft, whispery and full of fear. "This armour belonged to the very first Lord Crumbly," she explained. "He spent most of his time fighting wars. One morning, just before a big battle, he left his tent to go jogging. While he was away his arch-enemy Prince Nosechopper crept in and stole the armour. He put it on to fight and he was just charging into battle with his soldiers when the curse started. The suit suddenly began to work like a giant magnet, so anything that was made of metal got pulled towards it. Prince Nosechopper was buried under a pile of his own soldiers, with their helmets and swords stuck to his armour! Then the magnet began to work the opposite way, so the soldiers flew off him in every direction, like an explosion. They were so angry that they forgot about the battle and chased Prince Nosechopper, seeking revenge for making them look so stupid. He had to hide in a pile of cow manure for three weeks, and then it took him another three years to get rid of the smell of cow poo."

"Forget the armour, Ernie," the hairy burglar hissed.

"If I were you, I'd take that. It's worth thousands," Daisy said, pointing to an empty tin can that somebody had kicked into a corner.

"But that looks tiny," the burglars declared disbelievingly.

"It's a helmet that belonged to the famous midget Tom Thumb," Daisy whispered behind her hand, as if it was a very great secret.

"Then it's going in our sack!" the burglars chuckled happily. "Show us more! We want treasure!"

So Daisy took them up and up and up the winding stairs to the highest, spookiest tower in the whole castle.

"This is the Jewel Tower. It's stuffed full of riches," she promised.

"Just what we want!" the greedy burglars declared happily.

"The tower is haunted, of course. But I'm sure brave men like you don't care about that," Daisy remarked.

"Um, well..." the hairy burglar muttered nervously, taking a step backwards.

"Who haunts it exactly?" the bald burglar asked, suddenly looking pale.

"Well, let's see," Daisy mused, counting on her fingers. "There's the Eerie Earl, the Mad Marchioness, the Loopy Laird and the Desperate Duke. Horrible, horrible ghosts, all of them. One carries his head underneath his arm. One has got fangs. One screams and turns your blood cold and one has got worms instead of hair. But you won't mind, will you? You'd do anything to get that treasure, surely?"

Daisy opened the tower's creaking door a little way and at the same time she flicked a marble out of her pocket. It clattered down the stairs, all 300 of them.

"It's the ghosts! The horrible, horrible ghosts!" the burglars screamed, and they rushed down the stairs as fast as they could go, with their sack bumping and slithering down behind them.

They ran through the castle gardens and out of the front gate, but they didn't get far. Daisy made a phone call to the police, who soon arrived outside.

The burglars tried to hide in a bush, but the rubbish they had collected in their sack made the spot so smelly that a crowd of flies hovered overhead, and the police found them easily.

They were arrested for being a smelly danger to the public, and were taken away to hospital for a head check-up after they kept insisting that their sackful of garbage was treasure given to them by a little girl who lived in the castle.

When the police knocked on the castle door, no one answered. The police weren't surprised because they knew that nobody had lived there for many years.

Daisy, meanwhile, having protected her beloved castle, had gone back to

playing in its secret spidery rooms, which is just what little ghost princesses like to do best!

People still visit Crumbly Castle to look around. Perhaps you will one day. You won't mind the odd ghost, will you? You wouldn't be too scared to go into the Jewel Tower...would you?

Stan's Sundae Secret

Award-win
made with ou
very own secret in

Amy always knew when it was four o'clock in the afternoon because every day, come rain or shine, Manzoni's ice-cream van arrived and parked in the street opposite her bedroom window.

The van was brightly painted and the words 'Manzoni's ice-cream' were written across the front. On the side it had the words: 'Award-winning ice-cream made with our very own secret ingredient!'

As the van parked, it always played a tune through a speaker. Amy's mum had told her that the tune was from an Italian opera. Then Stan, the van owner and ice-cream-making genius himself, slid open the

window on the side of the van and stood
ready to serve his customers.

"Stan's ice-cream is famous, you know
– it's been on TV," Amy's mum would say.
"It's his secret ingredient that does it. I
don't know what they'd say at the diet club
if they knew I'd had one of his sundaes
yesterday. I just can't resist them."

Because of the opera tune and the
name Manzoni, everyone thought that Stan
was Italian. He didn't have an Italian
accent, but then he'd been living in Amy's
town for years now. He'd probably lost it
over time, Amy thought. She liked to
imagine him as a young man, sailing a
gondola around Venice in Italy, then one
day discovering the secret ingredient for
making the world's best ice-cream, maybe
in an ancient secret book he'd found.

Amy liked imagining adventures for
people she knew, and making them

exciting, like a movie. She loved films, and wanted to make movies when she grew up. In her imaginary tale about Stan, he was forced to run away from Italy by an evil gang who wanted to steal his ice-cream secret. But he had escaped on a boat to England.

The only problem was, Amy hadn't yet thought of a good ending for 'Stan's Adventure'.

One afternoon, Amy was buying her usual ice-cream cone from a smiling Stan, when a mysterious thing happened. Stan was just scooping some ice-cream out of a box when he froze, his hand in mid-air. A look of panic came into his eyes as he stared out past Amy's shoulder. She turned and saw a man in a black suit at the far end of the street.

Stan dropped his ice-cream scooper.

"Sherry!" he whispered to a startled

Amy. Then he slammed the van window shut, rushed to the driving seat and started the engine. The tyres screeched, just like they do in films. Stan was making a getaway!

Amy had no idea what was happening. All she knew was that the man in the black suit had scared Stan so much that, out of the blue, he had told Amy his secret.

"Sherry," he'd said. Amy didn't know what sherry was, exactly, but it must be part of Stan's secret.

"He's entrusted it to me!" she thought excitedly.

Suddenly the man in the black suit came up behind her.

"Young lady, was that the Manzoni van?" he asked. Amy thought fast. She mustn't give anything away! He was obviously Stan's enemy.

"I mustn't talk to strangers," she said, quickly turning and running home. Peeping out from behind a curtain, she saw him shake his head, walk back to his car and drive away.

As soon as he was gone, Amy rushed next door to find her friend Liam.

"Stan's run away!" she told him breathlessly. "I saw it. A man came and Stan rushed off! I think he's in big trouble."

"Maybe he was just late for something," he suggested.

"You don't understand. He told me his secret!" Amy insisted.

"What secret?" Liam asked.

"His secret ingredient. You know, the thing that makes his ice-cream so special," she explained.

"Oh, that!" Liam suddenly understood and looked much more interested. "My dad says it's probably a horrible chemical that Stan has got us all addicted to."

"Don't be stupid. Stan's a good guy. It's the other people who are horrible. The ones who are after him for his secret! Now I know it, too."

"They'll be after you, then," Liam sat forward and looked at her eagerly, but she realized from the look on his face that he didn't believe what she was saying. He thought it was a game and she was pretending they were in a movie.

"This could be serious, Liam," she insisted. "But we've got one advantage. The baddies don't know that I know the secret, yet."

"Which is...?" Liam added.

"Umm...I don't think I should tell you." She shook her head and Liam looked annoyed.

"Come off it, Amy. At four o'clock tomorrow Stan will be outside as normal," he said, refusing to play her game any more.

But the next day, at four o' clock, the street was empty. For the first time anybody could remember, Manzoni's ice-cream van did not arrive. Amy and Liam stood on the corner, with no ice-creams.

"I told you something was wrong! He'd be here if he could," Amy muttered. Before Liam could answer, she pushed him down behind a hedge.

"Quick, hide!" she cried.

They both peered out as a young, thin man with spiky hair strolled along the path.

"That's just Colin from the Crockpot

Café. Why are we hiding?" Liam asked.

"He's a suspect," Amy hissed. "He serves ice-cream in his café, doesn't he?"

"Well, yeah. But it's not very nice, nothing like Manzoni's," Liam remarked.

"Exactly. He'll be desperate for Stan's secret ingredient. He could be in a gang with the man in the suit," Amy whispered, but not quietly enough. Colin heard their voices and peered at them over the top of the hedge.

"What are you two up to?" he asked curiously.

"Nothing. Just playing," Amy replied rather too quickly.

"Where's the Manzoni van? I wanted a cone," Colin asked.

"He's not here," Liam blurted out too loudly. Amy was making him nervous.

Had Colin noticed how odd they both sounded? He didn't seem to. He shrugged and walked away.

Liam bobbed up.

"Liam, you idiot! Duck down! Here comes another suspect!" Amy cried.

"What? Mrs Rigg? She runs the diet club, doesn't she?" Liam replied, and failed to hide quickly enough as a determined-looking lady marched over and looked straight at them.

"Have you seen Manzoni's ice-cream van? I'm supposed to have a meeting with Stan," she demanded.

"He's away today. Why do you want to know?" Liam asked, trying not to sound so nervous this time.

Mrs Rigg frowned. "What a nuisance. I wanted to know exactly what he puts in his ice-cream," she sighed. "A lot of the ladies in my diet club are eating it, you see. I need to know the exact ingredients so I can work out how fattening it is." She bustled off, disappointed.

"She's dying to know his secret ingredient, too!" Liam whispered. He was beginning to think that perhaps Amy had stumbled onto something after all.

"Let's check out Colin, first," Amy said. But Liam didn't move.

"Look, if I'm going to help, I need to know the secret ingredient," he declared.

"Oh, all right then," Amy agreed and whispered it in his ear, "Sherry."

"Right," Liam said, not daring to admit that he had no idea what sherry was.

They walked down an alleyway that took them to the back of some shops in the next street. The Crockpot Café was at the end of the row. Colin's old car was parked outside, next to a back door and a back window made of frosted glass.

They crouched behind the car and waited. Suddenly they froze as shadowy outlines appeared behind the grimy window pane. One of them had Colin's spiky hair-shape. It looked as if he was holding a length of rope. The other outline was harder to make out.

"He's kidnapped Stan! He's tying him up!" Amy whispered. Her stomach flipped over. This wasn't the way she'd expected 'Stan's Adventure' to go!

They ran home and hid behind the shed in Amy's garden to talk about what they'd seen.

"We should go to the police," Liam urged.

"Without proof? They'll think we're just stupid kids," Amy replied.

"I could borrow my brother's camera.

We could go back and take a photo of Stan trapped behind the café window. That would be proof," Liam suggested.

Amy's mum appeared from around the corner and made them both jump.

"Liam, it's time for you to go home now," she said. "Are you OK? You both look pale."

Amy gulped. Maybe it was time to tell an adult, after all.

"Stan, the ice-cream man, has been kidnapped by Colin from the Crockpot Café. He wants Stan's secret ingredient. Mrs Rigg, your diet teacher, might be in on the plan," she explained, all in a rush.

Her mum nodded. "That sounds a very exciting story. Maybe you should write it down as one of your film scripts," she said. Amy sighed. Her mum wasn't going to take it seriously. No adult would without concrete evidence.

Then Liam piped up unexpectedly.

"What's sherry?" he asked.

Amy's mother looked startled. "Er, well, it's an alcoholic drink," she said.

"Really? But children can't have alcohol, can they?" Liam replied, looking puzzled.

"Absolutely not! That would be against the law," Amy's mum replied. "Off you go then, Liam."

"Bring the camera tomorrow," Amy mouthed silently as Liam left, looking very confused.

That evening Amy lay in bed unable to

sleep. Why was Stan mixing his ice-cream with alcohol, something that children weren't allowed to have? Had she got it all wrong? Was he a bad guy, after all? And if that was true, why had Colin kidnapped him? Who was the man in the black suit and what about the diet woman?

Next morning, Liam called early for Amy.

"I've borrowed the camera," he told her, taking it out from under his hoodie.

"I think we should take one photo, and then go straight to the police and let them take over," said Amy.

"OK, just one," Liam nodded. "But we need to be really careful."

They crept back to the Crockpot Café, keeping a wary eye out to make sure nobody was following them. They could just see the top of a head shape behind the window pane.

"It'll be Stan, tied up," Amy whispered. "You get a photo. I'll keep lookout."

Liam crept up close to the window. He put the camera up to his eye and pointed it through the frosted glass, then stumbled backwards and let out a scream as the shadow leapt at the window! A furious barking noise came from behind the glass.

The back door was flung open and Colin came out shouting at them. He would have grabbed Liam but, as he reached out, a large brown puppy bounded out of the café through his legs and tangled him up in its lead.

"Run!" Amy cried. Liam scrambled up off the floor and they fled.

They made it back to their street, sprinting all the way, and crouched down behind the hedge to get their breath back. If they'd been less shaken they would have chosen a better hiding place. As it was,

Colin found them easily. The puppy rushed up the street and sniffed excitedly at the hedge.

"Are you in there, you two?" he asked. They froze.

"Listen, I can explain about the dog," he whispered. "It's Brutus, my new puppy. I know I shouldn't keep him in the back of the café. But I can't leave him. He goes barmy when he's on his own. It's only temporary. Please don't tell anyone. The Health Inspector will close the café down if he finds out."

"You mean, you haven't got Stan tied up in your back room?" Liam demanded, standing up.

"Shut up, Liam!" Amy hissed. She still thought Colin could be lying.

"Eh? Stan in my back room? What are you on about?" a puzzled Colin asked.

Then Mrs Rigg appeared behind him.

"Colin, can we have a meeting to talk about the calories in your fried bacon sandwiches? I need to ask for my diet ladies, you see. I was going to sort out Stan's ice-creams first, but he's gone off to the coast for a break."

"The coast?" Liam repeated.

"Yes, dear. He rang me to say he was sorry he'd missed our meeting and he'd be back tomorrow. I'll come round to the café in about an hour, Colin," she announced, and marched off.

"Remember what I said, kids. Don't tell anyone about Brutus in the back room. I'll give you both a free milkshake," Colin winked and led Brutus away.

"So Stan has gone on holiday, and the only thing in Colin's back room is Brutus," Liam frowned.

"So they say," Amy snapped, unwilling to believe that she could have got everything about 'Stan's Adventure' so wrong. After all, why had Stan told her his secret? Why had he run away from the man in the black suit, and was he really putting alcohol in his ice-cream?

"I still think Stan's in trouble!" she insisted to Liam, who shook his head.

"We'll know tomorrow, at four o'clock," he snapped. He was feeling really fed up. He'd been half scared to death, and all for nothing.

The next day they sat in Amy's bedroom, trying to play a computer game but not really concentrating. Amy kept glancing nervously at her watch. She knew that Liam didn't believe her any more. He thought she'd made up the whole thing about the sherry and the man in the suit.

She might still be proved right, or be left looking daft. It all depended on what happened at four o' clock. Actually, it was five minutes to four when they heard the sound of the Manzoni ice-cream van.

"Surprise, surprise. Stan's back," Liam commented, looking sideways at Amy.

They went outside and walked towards the van. Stan looked down at them from his window, smiling.

"Hello, kids," he began, and then his eyes travelled to a point somewhere behind them. Amy spun around. It was the man in the black suit! He was standing in the road looking at Stan, who stared back at him. It was like a scene in a wild west movie, when two cowboys were about to have a shootout. Only this time the children were trapped between the two!

Stan broke the silence by letting out a sigh.

"Sherry?" he asked. The man nodded. He put his hand in his jacket pocket and pulled out, not a gun, but a letter.

"She's gone, but she wrote this before she died. She wanted you to have it," he explained and handed over the letter to Stan, who read it silently.

"It's been too long, too long," he muttered. He climbed out of the van and, to Amy's amazement, he hugged the man in the black suit.

"But...but...who is he?" she heard herself blurting out. Stan glanced down at her.

"This is my brother," he smiled. "How are you, Fred?" he asked, his voice breaking with emotion.

"I'm well, Stan. Very well. Good to see you," the man replied, smiling.

"Tell you what, Fred. I'll be with you in a minute. I'll just serve my two best customers here," Stan declared, and hopped back into his van.

"These are on the house," he said. He gave the children two ice-cream cones, then noticed that they weren't licking them.

"What's up?" he raised an eyebrow.

Liam whispered back, embarrassed.

"We can't eat your ice-cream because of the sherry. We're not allowed."

"What?" Stan scratched his head.

"Your secret ingredient. You know, the sherry. It's alcoholic so we can't have it," Liam replied.

"My secret ingredient is just some extra

milk powder I put in the ice-cream mixture," Stan remarked casually. He didn't seem to mind anyone knowing.

"Oh," Liam went bright red and glanced furiously at Amy.

"I think you're a bit confused. Sherry was my grandmother," Stan explained.

"In Italy?" Amy asked.

"I'll tell you a secret," Stan chuckled, leaning towards them. "I'm not really from Italy. I let people think I am because, well, it sells more ice-cream. I'm from Birmingham and my surname's Wiggins. My grandmother had a business up there. She never understood why I wanted to make ice-cream and not work for her. I fell out with the family about it and haven't spoken to any of them in years. When I saw my brother arrive here the other day I panicked. It all came back to me – all the rows and the heartache. I ran away, not for the first time. I had a little break at the seaside and I thought about things. I realized it was no good hiding from it all."

He looked fondly at his brother.

"Fred came to tell me that Sherry, my grandmother, passed away recently. But before she died she wrote me this letter. Her last wish was to end the family row."

Liam was listening so intently he didn't notice that his ice-cream was beginning to melt.

"Eat up now," Stan urged him and then turned to his brother. "Would you like a strawberry sundae, Fred?" he asked.

Amy and Liam wandered back home, thoughtfully licking their ice-creams.

"My imaginary 'Stan's Adventure' was OK," Amy thought to herself. "But the new one – the real-life truth about him – now that is an amazing story! I must write it down!"

Top Secret

S ome years ago, I won't say exactly when, a large spaceship zoomed towards Earth and hovered over a small town (I won't say which one). The ship had an invisibility shield all around it, so nobody would notice it. It came from Crangon, a faraway planet that no human knows anything about.

The Chief Engineer on board the Crangon spaceship spoke through one of his three alien mouths: "Co-ordinates set for Earth. Spaceship invisibility shield on. Spy mission cleared for landing."

"Ah, good," the captain replied, waving his antennae politely. His name was Captain Cribble, and he was the bravest, most fearless Crangonite ever.

"It's time for me to make my speech," he declared, and he stood up on his three legs to address the rest of his purple-headed space crew:

"We will soon be the first Crangonites ever to land on the miserable little planet they call Earth. Our mission is to spy on the humans who live there, to find out if they are strong fighters and what their weapons are. Once we know this we can make successful plans for a full-scale invasion. At our signal, the Crangon interplanetary army will send 1,000 spaceships and conquer Earth to use as a rubbish dump! Ha, ha, ha!"

Actually, what he said was: "Blar, blghkpk, ping," which was Crangon language, but we needn't go into that.

So here's the picture. This spaceship I mentioned was full of aliens with a bad attitude towards Earth. They were going to spy on humans to plan for an invasion later on by lots of other Crangonites, who needed somewhere to dump their old rubbish.

The aliens knew they wouldn't get very far on Earth if they stayed looking like they normally did (multiple mouths, purple knobbly skin and – this will shock you – their brains hanging out on the end of stalks). Looking so unusual, they knew they would soon be zapped by hostile Earth forces or possibly given a job in a boy band.

Luckily, Crangonites have the ability to change, or 'morph', into any shape they want. The spies on board this particular spaceship morphed into humans, only with no clothes on. That was no good, obviously, unless they landed in a nudist camp. They had to get dressed up, and they had brought some specially made clothes with them.

This is all quite true, by the way. You won't have heard about it because it was kept top secret. Only a few vitally important people, such as me, know the truth.

The Crangonites wanted to dump garbage such as broken zplargs, worn-out scrack regenerators and old skins. The Crangonites throw away their old skin and get a new one every birthday. They have six birthdays a year, so that's a big pile of unwanted skins when you think about it.

"Has everybody morphed?" Captain Cribble asked.

"I don't like my ears," someone complained.

"Should I have these hairs on my nose?" someone else asked worriedly.

Nobody was very happy being human-shaped because Crangonites thought it was an appallingly ugly look.

"We will now put on our human clothes," Captain Cribble announced. A picture flashed onto a space-optic video screen above their heads, showing what their clothes would look like. Scientists on the planet Crangon had been intercepting Earth TV for a while, and they had copied the clothes they had seen, ready for the spy mission. Unfortunately for the spies, Crangon was a very long way away from Earth. The only TV programme the scientists had picked up was a pop music show that took 20 years to reach them. This meant that the alien spies had been given fashions that were tragically out of date.

"Everyone, put on your lime-green high-waisted golf trousers," Captain Cribble ordered.

"Done," the crew confirmed.

"Now put on your pink sequinned disco shirts, and tuck them in, please."

"Done."

"Now your brown and yellow spotted socks with your plastic platform boots."

"Done."

The aliens looked truly sad. This lack of style needn't have been a problem if they had landed, say, at a parents' party or a teachers' get together. However, fatally for them, they had chosen to land on the football pitch of a school, just as the kids were coming out at the end of the day.

Before he sent his crew off on their mission, Captain Cribble gave them one final warning: "You all have personal invisibility shields. You may use them if you get into deep trouble," he explained. "But only do so if you absolutely have to. The shield will drain your powers and leave you too weak to fight or to morph back to your Crangon shape. One more thing. Please keep in contact with the spaceship over your radio mike. We need to know what it's like out there. Now go! Spread out and start spying! Be brave! Be fearless! I'll stay here and guard the door."

"Look! There is a crowd of humans! Let's follow them," the aliens cried excitedly, pointing at the children as they streamed out of school. The aliens all morphed down to the size of children, which made their clothes look very baggy and even sillier than before, if that was possible.

One of the aliens shuffled into a nearby sweet shop and stood behind some children buying sweets and comics.

"She's cool," one of the kids said, pointing to a picture of a pop star on the front of a magazine.

"I will copy this human and it will make friends with me. Then I can find out what weapons it has," the alien thought cunningly. He pointed to a picture of a famous male footballer on the cover of a magazine.

"She's cool," he said loudly.

One or two children looked around in puzzlement at the disguised alien.

"This is working well," he thought. He pointed to an old man who had just come into the shop to buy a newspaper.

"She's cool," he said.

"Eh? What?" the man spluttered. "Why, you rude little urchin!"

All the children in the shop turned and stared at the disguised alien. "Oh...er," he stuttered. He began to feel scared and ducked behind the sweet counter in case the staring humans were focusing some kind of laser eye weapon on him.

Then one of the children took out a mobile phone. When he saw it the alien panicked completely. He screamed into his radio mike: "The human has some kind of ray gun! This is an emergency. It is going to zap me!" As a last resort he activated his personal invisibility shield and disappeared from view. He crawled back weakly towards the Crangon spaceship as his powers drained away.

Outside, another alien spy was sitting on a bench listening to some schoolgirls talking.

"I'm going to get a new top," one of the girls said.

"A new top?" the alien thought worriedly. "Can the humans morph the top parts of their bodies? This could be serious for us."

"I'm going to change my hair," said another girl.

The alien gasped and spoke hurriedly into his radio mike: "It definitely sounds as if the humans can morph! They are much more powerful than we had thought!"

One of the girls got out a hairbrush. When the alien saw it he went cold with fear.

"I have found a human who is heavily armed. It has what looks like a photon-frying weapon, covered with lethal poisonous spikes!" the alien whispered urgently. Then the girl took out a pot of hair gel, and the alien leapt up with a yelp.

"The human has some high-action acid burning gunk! I am in terrible danger!" he squealed. "I must retreat! Retreat!" He activated his personal invisibility shield and staggered back towards the spaceship, his powers all but gone.

Meanwhile a group of alien spies was watching some children kicking a football around in the park.

"Shoot!" one of the children cried. The aliens all panicked, ducked and immediately used their invisibility shields. They too struggled back to the spaceship, blubbering into their radio mikes:

"I want to go home!"

"I've never met such horrible lifeforms!"

"What's going on?" Captain Cribble demanded, as his crew crept back through the door of the spaceship, wailing and hardly able to walk.

"The humans are armed and

dangerous, and they can morph!" one alien sobbed.

"They have ray guns and photon-frying weapons. What chance do we have?" another alien added in a terrified squeak.

"And they have a giant bullet which they call a football. It shoots out of their foot," another one blubbed.

"You weaklings!" Captain Cribble shouted. "I don't believe you! I have seen none of these things on their jolly TV programme, only happy harmless humans dancing and singing."

"It's true! It's true! We can't go back out there! Don't make us!" the crew begged.

But Captain Cribble was a true intergalactic hero. He had spent three giga-years in the army, learning defence and attack, interspace driving and antennae self-control. He didn't give up so easily.

"I will go myself, you useless shameful cowards. You are a disgrace to Crangon! Listen to me on the radio to learn how spying should be done!" The captain morphed into the shape of a schoolchild and stepped bravely out of the invisible spaceship onto the school football pitch.

"Hey! You can't walk there," the school caretaker immediately shouted at him. "Can't you read? There's a sign saying 'Keep off the grass'! I'll tell the Headteacher about you!"

Captain Cribble was not expecting an attack so early, but he remembered his Crangon army training and reacted quickly.

"I am moving away from a human who

appears to be very aggressive," he muttered into his radio mike, and he ran off the football pitch straight into the Headteacher himself.

"You, boy! Look where you're going!" the Headteacher roared in his best child-scaring voice.

Captain Cribble was startled. "But I won't give up, not yet," he insisted bravely. He backed away from the Headteacher, who was looking at him very suspiciously.

"This must be the powerful leader of the humans. His stomach is much larger than the rest of the tribe and his head is smooth and shiny," the captain muttered into the radio mike. "I think it would be a good idea to kidnap him and remove his brain for study."

"What's the matter with you? Are you planning some kind of mischief, boy?" the Headteacher asked.

"This leader has mind-reading powers! He will discover all the Crangon plans! I must get away!" Captain Cribble gasped. He ran off as fast as he could, which was not very fast due to his platform boots. Luckily he was faster than the Headteacher, whose stomach was so large that he could no longer run anywhere and had forgotten how to.

By the time he stopped running the fearless hero Captain Cribble found himself in a street near the school. Two children on bicycles were riding towards him.

"Incoming attack!" he cried and stepped backwards, bumping into an old lady who was standing at the bus stop.

"How dare you, young man!" she snapped and poked him with her rolled umbrella.

"The human has some kind of stabbing wand! I may have only minutes to live!"

Captain Cribble screamed down the radio mike.

"You stupid boy," the old lady muttered. Then her small dog appeared from behind her, growled at Captain Cribble and made a disgusting smell because it had eaten too much dog food that morning.

"Now they've used some kind of chemical weapon. I must escape!" Captain Cribble choked. He staggered through a door into a café full of computer games and fruit machines.

"I've found some kind of command

centre," he whispered eagerly into his radio mike. He crept up behind a group of children who were crowded round a machine, with a flashing title picked out in lights on the top. It was a computer game called 'Space Invasion 3000'. Captain Crangon knew nothing of computer games and thought the children were watching TV.

"Yeah! Zap the aliens!" the children cried as one of them pressed a button and a cartoon spaceship exploded on the screen.

"It's a disaster!" Captain Cribble groaned. "It looks as if the Crangon invasion has been started without us! It's being shown on Earth TV. Those poor Crangonite warriors. They have no idea what they are up against. The humans have so many powerful weapons to destroy them."

"Yes! We won!" the children cried, as several spaceships blew up together on the screen.

"Aaargh! The entire Crangonite fleet has been wiped out!" Captain Cribble gasped and, howling miserably, he ran back out into the street.

"That kid was weird," one of the children remarked. "He was wearing cool clothes, though. Brown and yellow spotted socks have just come back into fashion."

Meanwhile, unaware that his socks were once again trendy after 20 years, the shattered Captain Cribble rushed back towards the school football pitch, only to find that his terrified and cowardly crew had taken off without him.

"Come back! I command you!" he screamed into his radio mike.

"No way! We're going home," they replied, and cut him off.

He was trapped and unable to escape. In addition, he had forgotten to use his personal invisibility shield and now it was too late. He felt a human hand grip his shoulder.

"It's you again, boy," the Headteacher hissed into his ear. "You are going to get lots and lots and LOTS of detention."

From then on brave heroic Captain Cribble was stuck on planet Earth, with no way back home. Worse still, he found he no longer had the power to morph back to his original Crangon shape, so he had to stay looking like one of the incredibly ugly human children.

Gradually, over time, he learned to fit in, hiding his true identity. He continued spying on humans, in case his Crangon relatives ever decided to invade again. He discovered why the spying mission had gone so wrong, finding out that mobile phones were not ray guns, hairbrushes weren't photon-frying weapons and lime-green high-waisted golf trousers would never be trendy again, not in a million years.

Eventually he grew larger, as humans do over time. He is still forced to live on Earth and he is currently pretending to be someone by the name of...I can't say who because it's a secret and not even the government knows about it. I do, obviously, because I've just told you about it...Not that I'm Captain Cribble, you understand. Of course I'm not. The very idea! Why, I've never been to Crangon and have certainly never seen its purple volcanoes or its green gas seas. I don't know the first thing about it...

From the publisher: We apologize for this story being unfinished. Unfortunately the author has disappeared, and on his desk we found this note from the government, so...um...we suggest you read the next story. Sorry.

OFFICIAL NOTICE

This author has been taken away for questioning.

Signed: Department for Hunting Illegal Space Aliens.

The
Flying Pig

M ost pigs are happy with a normal, snuffling, munching kind of life. They may moan about the size of their dinners. They may wish they had more wallowing-in-the-mud time. But on the whole they are happy being pigs.

Puggle wasn't like that. He enjoyed his dinner as much as any young pig. But that was the only thing he liked about life on the farm. When his father showed him, with natural piggy pride, the proper way of rooting out turnips, Puggle shook his little pink head.

"I might get my nose dirty," he said.

Puggle's father paused. He could

hardly believe his ears. I mean, pigs *like* getting dirty, don't they? Noses, tummies, trotters and tails are always covered in mud. Rooting for turnips is quite a clean and tidy job! The older pig decided that he simply hadn't made himself clear.

"You see, son," he said, raising his voice a little and talking very slowly, "turnips are good to eat. Mmmm! Yummy! And to get them out of the ground, you have to shovel about with your snout, like this. Mmmnnfffmmm! See? It's fun! It's something pigs are good at. Rooting, that is. Now, you have a go."

"No, thank you," said Puggle. He had always been a polite little pig.

Mr Pig tried again. "It's not a case of 'No, thank you', Puggle," he said, a little more sharply. "This is something that all pigs do. And you will do it too. In fact, you will do it now. Get rooting!"

Puggle knew he had to do what he was told, so he rooted. But he really didn't enjoy it. (And he hasn't liked turnips ever since.) Mr Pig sighed. Why couldn't Puggle be like the other piglets? What was wrong with him?

The same thing happened when Mrs Pig tried to teach her son how to wallow in not-quite-wet-enough mud.

"You have to wiggle on your back a bit more," she explained, "which you don't have to do if the mud is really slurpy. Look, like this!"

And she wallowed very well.

"Now it's your turn, Puggle," she smiled. "This will be a real treat."

But Puggle just looked down at the puddle in front of his trotters and twitched his little pink nose.

"Do I have to?" he asked. "It doesn't seem very dignified, somehow."

"Dignified? Dignified? What on earth are you talking about?" squeaked his mother. She decided that Puggle must be a bit confused. Whoever heard of a pig wanting to be dignified? Pigs *like* rolling around in oozy mud, don't they?

"Wallowing is fun!" she explained. "Pigs are very good at wallowing. First on your back, then on your tummy – then roll in the squelchiest bit of the puddle, like this. Now, you have a go."

"No, thank you," said Puggle. (He really was a very polite little pig.)

"Have you been talking to the sheep?" asked Mrs Pig crossly.

Mr and Mrs Pig didn't like the sheep

out in the meadow. They had nothing to do all day but gossip, and they were quite likely to fill a young pig's head full of nonsense. Mrs Pig felt sure that was what had happened. After all, sheep are always scared of getting their coats dirty.

"Those silly sheep are nothing but trouble, Puggle," she told her son. "I don't want you talking to them any more. What do they know about being a pig? Now run off and play with the other piglets so I can wallow in peace."

Puggle was happy to escape into the farmyard, but he didn't go to play with the other piglets. The sooner he could get back to his experiments, the better.

You see, the reason that Puggle was not interested in rooting or wallowing was because he was *very* interested in flying. He had wanted to fly ever since he could remember. He thought about flying all day long, even when he was munching his dinner. At night, when other pigs dreamed about rooting and wallowing, Puggle dreamed about swooping through the blue sky (and sometimes he dreamed about dinnertime).

When he was a tiny piglet squiggling in the straw, he had been very excited by seeing a flock of swallows flying overhead. So animals could fly too! Puggle watched the swallows playing in the sky, looping the loop and having fun. He couldn't wait to start flying himself.

Puggle waited and waited for his wings to grow. He tried to be patient, and he filled in the time with lots of tasty food. But the hours between breakfast and dinnertime went very slowly for him. He knew that he was ready to start flying. But, of course, there was a problem. He wasn't ready. No pig was ready.

"Mother," he asked one day at breakfast. "When will my wings grow?"

Mrs Pig frowned and paused in her munching.

"Wings? What wings?" she said. "Honestly, Puggle, you do have some odd ideas. Pigs don't have wings, sweetheart."

"What, never ever?" asked Puggle. "Never, ever, ever?"

"Not ever," said Mrs Pig firmly. "It's a silly idea, Puggle. Pigs are too…er…plump to fly. A nice round pig couldn't get off the ground however many wings he had."

Puggle was very upset. He even left the rest of his breakfast. He had thought that it was only a matter of time before he would be soaring through the blue sky and the fluffy white clouds. Now it seemed as if it would only ever be a dream.

But, a few days later, Puggle was lying miserably under a tree when he heard a mother blackbird teaching her little baby birds how to fly.

"Now just remember," she chirped, "spread your wings nice and wide as you jump, and start flapping!"

This was news to Puggle. He thought birds knew how to fly as soon as they were born. But it seemed that birds had to learn to fly, just like he had learned to walk. As he listened to the mother blackbird, he felt hope rising inside him again. If bird-brained blackbirds could learn to fly, surely a super-clever pig could do it, with enough thought and practice?

The next few days were very painful for

Puggle. He tried to teach himself to fly by launching himself off higher and higher objects. When he jumped off the feed trough he only jolted his front trotters. Jumping off the sty wall gave him a badly bruised bottom. When he decided to jump off the sty roof he could have really hurt himself, but luckily it was a very good day for wallowing. Lots of pigs were wiggling and rolling in the slurpy mud puddle next to the sty. They were quite plump and squashy – so Puggle had a soft comfy landing. But his pride was hurt (and he got into trouble for bruising the elderly pigs).

Puggle even thought about jumping from the tree where the baby birds had been practising. He certainly had the courage to try it, but he soon found that trotters were not made for climbing tree trunks.

Once again, Puggle's dreams had been

crushed. He lay under the tree and moaned softly to himself (and that was only partly because of the badly bruised bottom).

Suddenly, high overhead, he heard a droning sound. It grew louder and louder and louder. Puggle looked up into the sky, but all he could see were big white clouds. A squirrel who lived in the trunk of the tree peered out of her hole crossly.

"What is it?" yelled Puggle. He had to yell, because the noise overhead was so loud.

"It's an aeroplane," shouted the squirrel. "Haven't you ever seen one before? They're very annoying, especially when I'm trying to get my babies to sleep. I can hardly hear myself think!"

Puggle waited a moment or two for the noise to die away.

"But what is it?" he asked. "I mean, what is an aeroplane? I know that it flies and it makes a lot of noise. Is it an animal? Does it do anything else? Does it ever come down to the ground?"

"I'm not sure," said the squirrel. "I don't think it's an animal. I think it's a machine, like a car. And I don't think it ever lands. I've never seen one on the ground. I think it drones about up there all the time."

When the squirrel had gone, and Puggle had a chance to think, he felt more hopeful. You see, pigs are a lot cleverer than squirrels, and the squirrel had said that an aeroplane was like a car. Puggle knew that cars carried people. Was it possible that aeroplanes carried people as well, only through the air instead of along the ground? Puggle thought about it while he was munching his dinner and, the more he thought, the more sure he felt that he was right.

That evening, one of the farm children

left a library book on the grass. Puggle had nibbled the cover and chewed a couple of pages before he noticed that the pictures in the book were all of flying machines. And the machines had people in them. Certainly, they were strange people, with helmets and scarves and huge goggly eyes, but then people were strange anyway, from a pig's point of view. Puggle looked very carefully at the pictures and was very sorry about the pages that were now inside him. He wished he could read the black squiggles. When he went to sleep that night his head was buzzing with ideas. For the first time, there seemed to be a real chance that he could fly.

The next morning, straight after breakfast, Puggle set to work to build a flying machine. It's surprising what you can find lying in the back of a barn if you look hard enough. Pretty soon, Puggle had found a large crate, a bicycle wheel, a plank of wood and lots of rope to tie everything together.

Trotters are not ideal for tying knots, but snouts are pretty good. Puggle worked very hard. He was so excited that he didn't even stop for dinner. He lifted and pulled, tied and knotted, and by the end of the day he had something that looked very like a plane. At least, it had a cockpit and wings, and the bicycle wheel on the front looked a little bit like a propeller.

Puggle knew that he should get a good night's sleep before starting on his great adventure. (And he wasn't quite sure how easy night flying was.) But this was too exciting to wait. If he was going to fly, he must do it now!

As the sun set behind the far fields, Puggle climbed into his flying machine. The moment he had dreamed of had come at last. Now all he had to do was to make the machine work.

He thought hard about flying. He imagined how it would feel to be up in the sky, swooping above the treetops. He waited for the machine to lift up into the air. But nothing happened. Puggle peered over the edge of the cockpit. He was still very near the ground. As near as you can get. He hadn't moved at all.

Puggle paused for thought. Of course! A machine needed to make a noise to work. The farmer's car and tractors made a terrible noise, and the aeroplane had made a really deafening sound.

"Brrrrrrrrrmmmmm!" cried Puggle. "Brrrrrrmm! Brrrmm! BRRRRMMM!"

The noise made the hens scatter and hide in the barn, and the ducks in the pond started quacking loudly. But nothing else happened. The plane didn't so much as jiggle. Poor Puggle felt his heart sink down to his trotters. After all his hard work, it was clear that his aeroplane wasn't going to fly. Sadly, he climbed out and set off for the sty, his tummy rumbling loudly. Flying was as impossible as ever.

Now Puggle was a lucky young pig, and not only because he had such an unusual mind. He also happened to be very good looking, and the farmer had decided to take him to the County Show. Mr and Mrs Pig were very excited. They had both won prizes at the show in the past, and now it was Puggle's turn. They felt sure he would make them very proud.

"Remember to keep your snout up," said Mr Pig.

"And show them your nice curly tail — that's what they like to see," added Mrs Pig.

"I'll remember," sighed Puggle, trying not to look at his flying machine in the corner of the farmyard.

Next day, the farmer gave Puggle a very thorough wash (including parts he didn't even know he had) and polished his trotters until they shone. Then he loaded Puggle, a sheep who looked as if she had been to the hairdresser's and a duck with bright white feathers into the back of his truck and set out for the local showground.

He felt pretty sure that Puggle would win a rosette.

Puggle rather enjoyed his wash and brush up. He liked the idea of seeing somewhere new too. After all, it would keep his mind off his flying career.

The showground was very busy, with lots of farm animals and farmers, all hoping to win rosettes. There were cows and sheep, hens and ducks – Puggle didn't know which way to look first!

Puggle did very well at the show. He won first prize and had a great many ladies in hats cooing over him and admiring his curly tail. It was very interesting to see all the people. But later in the afternoon, while the judges were looking at the sheep, Puggle became rather bored. So he lifted the latch of his pen with his clever little snout and set off to explore the showground. Perhaps someone in the crowd would have noticed that a pig was out of his pen, but at that moment a droning noise began to get louder and louder above them all. Everyone stared up at the sky.

Puggle couldn't see a thing among all the legs of the crowd, so he climbed up onto a bale of straw. The little pig could hardly believe his eyes! There was a *flying machine*, flying low enough for him to see the person inside. And the machine was looping the loop and doing all kinds of stunts, just like the swallows Puggle had seen when he was a tiny piglet.

Puggle's heart was thudding as the plane landed and the crowd cheered and clapped. As the pilot jumped out onto the field, the people rushed forward to meet him. He started to shake people's hands and sign their autograph books.

No one noticed a little pink shape

flashing across the field.

No one noticed the engine of the plane burst into life again.

Even when the plane began to move forward, slowly at first and then faster and faster, no one shouted.

It was only when Puggle pulled the throttle right back and the engines roared that the pilot stopped signing autographs and yelled out, "My plane!" He raced across the field.

But by then it was too late. The plane lifted smoothly into the air. Puggle grinned and waved a trotter to the people who were getting smaller and smaller below him. He felt wonderful! It was just as good as he had known it would be. He dived and he looped. He swooped and he swerved. He was born to fly and everyone could see it now.

At last, after he had looped the loop around one very fluffy white cloud, Puggle

started to steer towards his home. He flew over fields and woods, until he saw his own farm below. It seemed very, very far away. His pigsty was a tiny dot in the corner of the little farmyard. His feed trough was an even tinier dot. He remembered that it was dinnertime.

Puggle felt a pang. It hit him somewhere between his ribs in a place that he liked to keep full of something tasty.

Now, Puggle was an extraordinary pig, but he was a pig all the same. He suddenly realized that several hours had passed since breakfast. They had been exciting hours – amazing hours. But in all those wonderful hours, Puggle hadn't eaten a single scrap of food.

Puggle paused for a moment. Then he turned the aeroplane around and prepared to land.

In the great struggle between flying planes and eating dinner, there's really no contest…

Get Me Out of Here!

B en switched on the computer and it whirred into action.

"Here we go!" said Eric, taking a deep breath. The haunted house came up on screen. Everything looked the same as usual. The headless ghost paced up and down, moaning and wailing. The snake pit writhed and heaved in the basement. In the attic a million bats hung from the rafters, and in the deepest darkest dungeon Eric rattled the heavy chains that bound him to the wall.

"Help!" he cried. "Get me out of here!"

But Ben couldn't hear him.

Ben was mad about his computer. He used it all the time. He used it to do his homework. He used it to email his friends. And quite often he used it to play computer games. He was playing his favourite game now. It was called 'Get me out of here!'

In this game a boy called Eric was trapped in a haunted house. It was up to Ben to set him free. To do this Ben had to answer a lot of questions. If he got the answer right it helped Eric; if he got the answer wrong it didn't. Yesterday Ben had managed to get Eric out of the dungeon and past the pitful of snakes. But then he got an answer wrong and Eric was back in the dungeon where he started. Today, Ben was determined to do better.

He looked carefully at the screen. He could see Eric looking scared and fed up. Ben could understand why. If it was him chained up in the dungeon, he'd be scared and fed up. The first question flashed up on the screen.

WHAT IS THE CAPITAL OF FRANCE?

It was followed by four answers:

MADRID

PARIS

LISBON

LONDON

Next to each answer was a different coloured button. On Ben's control were the same buttons. This question was easy. The questions at the beginning were always easy – it was later on that they became difficult.

Ben pressed the red button for **PARIS**. A bell rang, and Eric burst out of his chains. Ben thought he looked relieved. The next move was to unlock the dungeon door. This time the question was a bit harder.

WHAT IS THE NAME OF THE STRETCH OF WATER BETWEEN ENGLAND AND FRANCE?

There was a choice of two answers:

THE ATLANTIC

THE ENGLISH CHANNEL

Ben thought for a moment then pressed the blue button for **THE ENGLISH CHANNEL**. The bell rang again, and Eric opened the dungeon door and walked out.

"I hate this," said Eric to himself, inching his way along the dark passage. "Somewhere along here is a pit of snakes, and unless Ben gets the next question right I shall fall smack into it like I did yesterday."

Eric really hated the pit of snakes. He hated it even more than he hated the slimy cold dungeon. "Why can't I be in a nice computer game?" he moaned. "Why can't I be marooned on a desert island with blue sea and white sand and palm trees, instead of here in this horrible haunted house?"

The third question came up on screen.

IS A WHALE A FISH OR A MAMMAL?

Ben looked at the choice of answers carefully. There were only two:

MAMMAL

FISH

He had to get this one right or poor Eric would end up in the snake pit.

"A whale must be a fish," thought Ben aloud. "It lives in the sea like other fish." He wasn't quite sure what a mammal was. He supposed it was an animal. "A whale can't be an animal, can it?" he said.

In the haunted house Eric held his breath while Ben hummed and ha-a-ed. Ben's finger hovered over the red button for **FISH** and then over the blue button for

MAMMAL. He couldn't make up his mind.

Dad came into the room.

"Dad," said Ben, "is a whale a fish or a mammal?"

"A mammal," said Dad.

"Brilliant," thought Eric. Ben pressed the blue button and Eric jumped over the snake pit. The snakes looked up and saw the bottoms of his feet and legs above their heads.

"We'll get you next time, Eric," they hissed loudly.

Now he was past the snake pit Eric found himself in a square room. There were no windows in the room, only four doors. A blue door, a yellow door, a red door and a black door. Eric knew this room well. He had been here before. The blue door led into a room full of spiders. Eric hated that room. The spiders' webs wrapped themselves around his face and the spiders tried to crawl inside his shirt.

The yellow and red doors were almost as bad. The yellow door led into a room where a ghost sat crying in a corner. Eric never knew what to say to cheer him up. The red door led into a witches' den where three witches chanted spells over a boiling cauldron. Two of the witches were covered in warts, and the other had a black moustache and a beard. Eric was scared they would turn him into a pork pie and eat him up.

Eric dreaded going into these rooms. The only chance he had of escaping was to go through the black door. He kept his eyes fixed on Ben's face as the next question came up on the screen.

WHICH AMERICAN PRESIDENT WAS ASSASSINATED IN 1962?

ABRAHAM LINCOLN

GEORGE W. BUSH

JOHN F. KENNEDY
GEORGE WASHINGTON

Eric saw Ben frown slightly.

"I don't like the look of that frown," he said to himself. "When people frown it means they don't know."

Eric was right. Ben was puzzled. He knew the answer wasn't George W. Bush. He was sure Bush hadn't been assassinated. He had seen him on the news only the other day making a speech about something or other. Ben wasn't really interested in politicians. Now, if the question had been about football, he was sure he could have answered it.

He frowned again. Inside the haunted

house, Eric groaned. It didn't look good. "He's going to get it wrong," he thought.

Ben's hands hovered over the range of buttons. At the back of his mind he had an idea that Lincoln had been assassinated while he was watching a play. The more he thought about it the more certain he became. Ben pressed the yellow button.

"No!" yelled Eric as the yellow door opened. He could see the ghost sitting in a corner. He was still crying. The ghost raised a finger, beckoning Eric to enter. Reluctantly Eric went in, and the yellow door shut behind him.

Ben felt really bad. "Hang on, Eric," he called, although he knew Eric couldn't hear him. "I'll have you out of there in a minute, I promise."

Eric did hear him. "Oh yeah!" he said, trying to keep as far away from the ghost as he could. "Oh yeah! Where have I heard that before?"

"Not from me, young fella-me-lad," said the weeping ghost. "Not from me. I like a bit of company, it cheers me up."

Back in the real world Ben waited as another question came up on screen. He had to get Eric out of that room. He just had to. He couldn't leave him there, all by himself, with that creepy ghost. He didn't know if he had imagined it, but this time Eric had looked really scared.

Ben looked carefully at the next question. At first glance it didn't seem too bad. At least it was about something he was familiar with – sport.

WHICH SPORT DOES TIM HENMAN PLAY?

The choice of answers was:

GOLF

TENNIS

Ben knew this one. With a feeling of

triumph he pressed blue for **TENNIS**. The yellow door opened and Eric hurled himself back into the windowless room with the four doors. "Thank you, thank you," he mouthed silently. Just then Ben's mother called, "Switch that computer off, Ben. It's late."

"Can I have a bit longer?" asked Ben. "I want to get Eric out of the haunted house before I go to bed."

"Eric can wait," said Mum. "You've got school tomorrow."

Eric couldn't believe what he was hearing. If Ben closed down the computer, he would have to go back to the beginning. "Just as I was getting somewhere," he fumed.

Ben looked at Eric's angry face. "Back tomorrow, Eric," he said, and closed down the computer.

But Ben didn't play the game the next

day. Something happened at school that made him forget all about Eric and the haunted house.

Because he had worked hard that term, Ben was chosen with five other children to go on a camping trip over the weekend. They had to put up their own tents and cook for themselves. Ben had often been on camping holidays with his mum and dad, and he had really liked it. He even had a small tent of his own which he sometimes put up in the garden. It was big enough for two people. He was going to share it with his friend Martin.

When they arrived at the campsite it

didn't take long to put up the four tents. The six children slept two to a tent, and their teacher, Mr Crossley, had a tent to himself.

The campsite was up in the hills a long way from anywhere. Being high up they could see for miles. The countryside stretched out in front of them, empty except for some farms and sheep. If they ran out of something they would have to manage without it.

That night it was Ben's and Martin's turn to do the cooking.

"Right boys," said Mr Crossley, "how about making spaghetti bolognese? I'm sure everyone likes that."

The children nodded. They were all hungry. Mr Crossley lit the camping gas stove. Ben and Martin looked at each other. Neither of them had done any cooking before.

"What do you do first?" asked Mr Crossley.

"Fry the mince and onions in olive oil," said Vanessa. Girls often know more about these things than boys.

"Then add the tomatoes," said Penny.

"Good," said Mr Crossley. And while the two boys prepared the dinner he told them how important it was to put garlic and herbs in the sauce as well. "It's my favourite Italian dish," he told them.

The spaghetti bolognese was really good. "I'll make it for Mum and Dad when I get home," Ben told Mr Crossley.

That night Ben slept well. He liked sleeping in a tent, it was so much more fun than in a bed. He was woken by Martin.

"Ben, wake up!" Martin whispered. "What's that weird noise?"

Ben sat up. It was dark inside the tent. He could just make out the shape of his friend inside his sleeping bag. Everything was very still and quiet.

"I can't hear anything," he said. "You must have been dreaming." Then he heard a snuffling noise, followed by heavy footsteps. His skin began to prickle.

"This is scary!" said Martin.

"It sounds like a small animal," said Ben.

"Wrong!" said Martin, his voice muffled from inside the sleeping bag. "It sounds like a BIG animal."

Ben switched on his torch and opened the flap of the tent. Dazzled by the light, something brown and prickly curled up into a tight ball.

"It's a hedgehog," said Ben with relief.

"It sounded like an elephant," said Martin, coming to look.

When they told Mr Crossley the next morning he explained that hedgehogs were nocturnal creatures, like owls and bats, and were just looking for food.

"Do you know what nocturnal means?" he asked.

Ben thought he knew. "Staying awake at night," he replied.

"And sleeping during the day," added Mr Crossley.

The rest of the trip went well. The children walked and fished and, at the end of the day, before crawling into their tents, they lay on the grass looking up at the night sky. Mr Crossley told them the names of the stars and planets.

While Ben was away on his trip, Eric

was getting really fed up.

"It's all right for him," he complained. "He's having a great time, and I'm stuck here." To pass the time he scratched on the dungeon wall, in big letters, BEN – GET ME OUT OF HERE!

When Ben switched on the computer, he had a surprise.

At first, he didn't notice anything different. There was Eric in the dungeon, chained up as usual. In the corridors the headless ghost moaned and wailed, and in the snake pit the snakes were pretending they didn't care whether Eric fell in or not. Everything looked as it always did.

And then Ben spotted some scratchy writing on the wall of the dungeon. He didn't remember seeing it before.

BEN, it said, GET ME OUT OF HERE! It was just to the right of Eric's head.

Ben stared at the writing, then he stared at Eric. Eric stared back. Just then the first question flashed on screen.

HOW MANY WEEKS ARE THERE IN A YEAR?

52

48

"52," said Ben, and pressed the button next to **52**. The bell rang and Eric sprang out of his chains.

The next question flashed up on the screen.

HOW MANY EGGS IN A DOZEN?

10

12

"Easy," thought Ben, "12," and he pressed the **12** button.

Eric unlocked the dungeon door. Then, before he went into the dark passageway, he turned to Ben and gave the 'thumbs up' sign.

"That's weird," thought Ben, "I don't think he's ever done that before."

Ben was playing the game well. He answered the next question correctly, and Eric jumped over the snake pit and entered the square room with the four doors. Ben got another question right and Eric went through the black door. He had never been this far before. He was so excited he couldn't stop grinning. Ben was grinning too.

On the other side of the black door was a choice of two passageways. One led Eric nearer to freedom and one was blocked by the headless ghost who walked endlessly up and down, carrying its head tucked underneath its arm.

Eric turned to face Ben. He looked him straight in the eye. Ben could see the anxiety on his face.

Up came the next question. It was a difficult one.

HOW MANY GRAMS IN A KILOGRAM?

There were two answers:

100 GRAMS

1,000 GRAMS

Ben wasn't sure. He would have to guess. He guessed wrong!

"100 GRAMS," he said, and went to press the red button.

"No, you idiot," yelled Eric, "press the blue one."

Ben was too surprised to argue. He pressed the blue button. The headless ghost wailed, "Doomed...doomed..." and Eric raised his arms above his head. Then he ran into the passageway that led to freedom.

But Eric hadn't escaped yet. In this passage was another pit. This one was full of skeletons. A question flashed up on screen.

WHICH VEGETABLE DO THE ITALIANS USE A LOT IN THEIR COOKING?

RADISH

CARROT

LEEK

GARLIC

Ben knew this, or thought he did. He had put garlic in his spaghetti sauce a few days ago, and that was Italian. He pushed the yellow button and a paving slab slid over the pit of skeletons. They rattled their bones in protest as Eric ran over them down the passage.

Now Eric was faced with an iron grid. Through it he could see shafts of daylight.

WHICH OF THESE ANIMALS IS NOCTURNAL? was the next question.

DOG

COW

HEDGEHOG

SHEEP

Eric was gripping the iron grill with his hands. "I don't know this one," he said to Ben.

"I do," said Ben. He couldn't believe

his luck. He smiled to himself as he thought of the night-time visitor to his and Martin's tent on the camping trip. Ben pressed the blue button for **HEDGEHOG**.

The iron grill lifted.

Now Eric found himself in an overgrown garden. There seemed to be a high stone wall all around it. On top of the wall were strands of barbed wire. The only way out was a massive wooden gate at the far end.

"You're nearly there, Eric," shouted Ben.

"I don't know why you're talking to Eric," said Mum, coming into the room. "He can't hear you."

Ben hid a smile. And Eric, from deep inside the walled garden, hid a smile too.

When Mum had gone out Ben whispered, "One more question."

"Make sure you get it right," answered Eric.

The last question came up on screen.

WHICH OF THESE IS THE NEAREST PLANET TO EARTH?

MARS

JUPITER

SATURN

MERCURY

Ben and Eric looked at each other. "I should know this," said Ben, and he told

Eric how he and his friends had looked at the night sky when they were camping. "Our teacher told us all about the planets and stars," said Ben.

"You were dead lucky," said Eric. "While you were looking at the stars, I was chained up in a dark dungeon."

"You're nearly out," said Ben. "I just have to get this question right."

"You'd better hurry," said Eric. "It's getting dark. I don't want to be out here on my own."

Ben looked at the screen. The sky was almost black. He could see the moon and a few stars. It looked familiar. It had looked a bit like that when he was camping.

Then he noticed that one of the stars had a red tinge to it.

"Wait a minute," he said to Eric. "That red star, is it Mars?"

"Don't ask me," said Eric. "I've never seen the sky before."

"I think that's the one," said Ben excitedly. "Mars is the one that's nearest to Earth."

"Press the button then," said Eric, "and get me out of here!"

"Good luck, Eric," said Ben, and pressed the red button for **MARS**.

It was the RIGHT answer.

On screen, Ben watched as the huge gates opened and Eric stepped through them into the big world beyond. Ben wondered where he was going, and whether he would be all right, but all he could see was the empty garden getting darker and darker as night fell.

Then there was a flash on the screen followed by another. The flashes were so bright that Ben put up his hand to shield his eyes. When he took his hand away a small figure leaped through the screen and landed in front of him.

It was Eric.

"Free at last!" he cried.

The Most Dangerous Dragon

A cold wind whistled around the castle. Ice covered the lake outside and the grass was hidden by a thick layer of white frost. The trees around the castle were bare. Inside, the hunting dogs were lying close to the fire in the Great Hall. Old Duncan Dobetter was sitting in a chair next to the fire. As usual, he was telling stories to the children. Duncan's stories were always about the same thing…dragons.

"A dragon is always dangerous," Duncan said, pulling his cloak closer around his shoulders. "But the most dangerous dragon of all is the invisible dragon. He could be with us now, here in this hall, and we would never know until it was TOO LATE!"

One of the lads listening to Duncan's story was called Stefan Stinkle. He had bright-red hair and a long, thin nose. He was very interested in what Duncan had to say. Stefan had been trying to think of a way of becoming rich and famous. Dragon slaying seemed like a good idea. But Stefan wanted to find out if old Duncan really knew what he was talking about.

"You know a lot of stories about dragons," said Stefan Stinkle, "but have you ever actually come face to face with one?"

"Let me tell you, young Stinkle," cried Duncan, "I've met more dragons than you could ever imagine. I could tell you a story that will make your hair stand on end."

Stefan smirked. "Go on then," he said. He thought Duncan was a silly old man.

The children came closer to the fire

and sat down around Duncan's chair. Duncan took a sip from the silver goblet in his hand. Then he started to speak in a quiet, deep voice.

"One day when I was young," he began, "my grandmother said that she had a big secret to tell me. She warned me that our family was under a curse. Every 20 years, one son was always killed by a dragon. 'It has been that way with the Dobetters,' she said, 'since the beginning of time, and it will be that way forever. I thought it was only fair to warn you, young Duncan, that you don't have long to live.'"

"But why did it have to be you?" asked one of the lads. "Couldn't it have been your brother or your cousin?"

"It could have been," said Duncan, "if I had had any brothers or male cousins. But I didn't. I had seven sisters and more girl cousins than I could count. There was no one else. If my parents didn't have more children, I would be killed by a dragon."

"And did they have more children?" asked Stefan Stinkle. He was getting quite interested. He had six sisters himself and he knew how it felt to be the only boy. He even felt a bit sorry for old Duncan.

"Yes, they did," said the old man. "They had four more children…and they were all girls. So I made up my mind to find out everything I could about dragons. If I had to be killed by a dragon one day, I wanted to know as much as I could about them. So I read all the books about dragons I could find. I talked to everyone I knew who had ever seen a dragon. In a very short time, I became an expert on every kind of dragon. It was quite fascinating."

"Why?" Stefan asked. He didn't like the sound of all that reading. "What is there to know?"

"Ah," old Duncan took another swig from his goblet. "There are a lot of things it is useful to know. For example, do you know how dragons are born?"

"Born? They're not born!" laughed Stefan. He thought Duncan was being very stupid. "They just *are*, like mountains and music. Dragons are always hundreds of years old!"

"Dragons who bother humans are usually hundreds of years old, yes," said Duncan, "but all dragons were young once, just like you and me. They hatch out of eggs, deep in the mountains."

"I've never heard of a dragon's egg,"

said Clarence. He gave a little shiver. "Why hasn't anyone ever seen one?"

"Because they are grey, like rocks, and very big. You have probably all seen them, but they just look like big, grey boulders to you."

"How big are baby dragons?" asked Marku.

"About as big as a cow," replied the dragon expert. "But they are very shy. Their mothers keep them deep inside a cosy cave until they are ready to start wandering around the countryside, looking for food."

"What do they eat when they are deep inside the cave?" asked Stefan. He wasn't sure he believed any of this, but he couldn't stop listening now.

"Anyone their mother brings back from her hunting trips," said Duncan.

"Anyone? But don't they eat cows and sheep and rabbits and things?" Marku asked. He had gone very pale.

"Only if they are very hungry," said Duncan. "Humans are the food they like best. Their favourite is people with red hair and long noses." Duncan looked at Stefan. "Did you say something, Stinkle?"

"Nothing," said Stefan, pulling down his helmet to cover his bright-red hair.

"I want to hear more about dragons," said Clarence. "You said that you had met them before. What happened? How did you escape?"

"The very first dragon that I met was that very dangerous kind I mentioned at the beginning. He was invisible, but absolutely deadly."

"If he was invisible, how did you know he was there?" Stefan still wasn't sure he believed Duncan's story.

Duncan frowned and looked Stefan in the eyes. "Believe me, Stinkle, when you are near to a dragon, *you know.* At least, you know if you have any brains at all.

"It happened like this.

I was walking through the woods one day when I began to notice a smell of burning. The day was cold and the leaves of the trees shut out the sun, but suddenly the air felt warmer. As I walked on, I noticed that patches of leaves and bits of tree trunks were black, as if they had been burned by a strong fire. I should have realized the truth then, but I didn't have the sense to see it. I just kept on walking."

"Could you hear the dragon?" asked Marku.

"No, the woods were silent. Not a single bird sang in the branches. There were no squirrels or little woodland creatures at all. That should have warned me, but it didn't. I walked on in the strange silence. Then suddenly I was in the middle of a thick fog."

"A fog? Like the one that comes across the fields and around the castle every morning?" asked Clarence.

"Exactly like that," replied Duncan with a smile. "This fog swirled around me in a very strange way. I kept thinking I could see shapes and shadows on the path, but there was never anything there. And the fog was warm, too, not cold and clammy like normal fogs. You see, the fog was really the breath of the dragon. It curled around the trees and surrounded me. I still didn't know that it was a dragon, but I was starting to feel very scared. For one thing, I knew that I was completely lost."

"You should have marked the trees," said Stefan. He liked telling people what they had done wrong. "Everyone knows that's what you should do if you can't find your way home."

"Perhaps you are right," said Duncan, "but I've never seen how that can help. It wouldn't stop you walking in a circle. It would just mean that you would *know* you were walking in a circle. Anyway, I didn't do it. I called out for help, and that was a big mistake."

"That's what I would have done," said Clarence.

"Thank you, Clarence. It did seem like a good idea at the time. And only a few seconds later it looked as if help had come. An old man came out of the fog. He was wearing a large grey cloak with a hood over his face. It seemed as if he just grew out of the thick grey fog, which was a bit scary. But the light can play strange tricks with your eyes, so I thought I had imagined it. I was so glad to have some help."

"But wasn't it spooky, when you couldn't see his face?" Clarence asked. He wasn't very brave.

"I didn't think of that then," Duncan explained. "I was just so happy to see another human being. I ran towards him, calling out that I was lost. But when I reached him, he raised his hooded head and I saw his terrible face."

"What was it like?" all the lads asked together.

Duncan didn't answer straight away. He shivered and took another drink from his goblet. After a long silence, he said, "What was really terrifying was that *there was no face*. The man in the cloak just had a dark black hole where his face should have been."

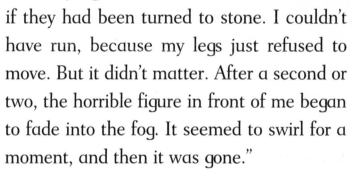

"Did you run away?" Clarence squeaked.

"My legs felt as if they had been turned to stone. I couldn't have run, because my legs just refused to move. But it didn't matter. After a second or two, the horrible figure in front of me began to fade into the fog. It seemed to swirl for a moment, and then it was gone."

"What a relief!" said Marku.

"I thought so too, at first," Duncan replied. He looked into the flickering flames of the fire. "But suddenly I felt more alone than I had ever been in my life. I was completely lost. I didn't dare to call for help again, in case the strange man in the cloak came back. And what happened next was even more frightening."

He sipped again from his goblet.

"Go on, go on!" The boys were desperate to know what had happened.

"The fog started to get even thicker," said Duncan, "and it suddenly got very, very hot. I could feel a burning on my neck and face. It seemed as though the fog was burning me."

"It was the dragon!" cried Clarence. He gave a little shiver.

"Yes, it was, but I still didn't know that. I only knew that I was absolutely terrified. My thoughts were whirling so fast in my head that I couldn't think of a single sensible thing to do. I was only a young boy then, and I started to cry. Tears streamed down my face as I stood there in the burning fog."

"And then?" said Stefan, laughing at old Duncan. Stefan thought that boys who cried were wimps.

"Suddenly my legs felt very weak," Duncan said. "I fell onto my knees and clutched the trunk of the nearest tree. But I did not feel the rough bark of the tree under my fingers. I felt smooth, shiny scales, like the skin of a snake. That was when I knew that I was dealing with a dragon. I knew that the end had come. My grandmother had said that one Dobetter son was killed by a dragon every 20 years. Now it was my turn."

Outside the castle, the wind howled even louder. There was silence in the Great Hall, except for the panting of the dogs.

The boys looked up at old Duncan with open mouths and wide eyes.

"What happened? How did you escape?" they cried, gazing eagerly at the old man. They were all scared by Duncan's story. All except Stefan Stinkle.

Stefan had a nasty look on his face. He still wasn't sure that he believed Duncan Dobetter's story. Worse still, he began to think that he didn't want to be a dragon-slayer after all. Duncan had escaped from the dragon he was telling them about. And, if he was telling the truth, it was not the only time he had met a dragon and escaped. Duncan Dobetter was not very clever, or brave, or strong. If a man like that could meet dozens of dragons and escape, it must be pretty easy. And something as easy as that would never make Stefan rich and famous. More than anything, Stefan wanted to be very, very rich. Suddenly, he felt Duncan's eyes watching him. The old man had a strange expression on his wrinkled face.

"Stefan," he said, "my old throat is dry.

I must have some more to drink before I go on with the story, but my goblet is empty. Please will you go down to the kitchens and fill it for me?"

"Oh, why me?" whined Stefan at once. He hated doing things for other people. "Why can't one of the others go?" But the old man just shook his head and held out his goblet. Stefan took it and set off for the kitchens. They were far below the Great Hall, in the deepest part of the castle.

Now, I expect you know very well that castles were not very comfortable places to live in. They were dark and cold. There was no glass in the tiny windows, and there was no central heating. The passages and stairways were freezing cold. The rooms with fires were stuffy and much too hot. The only good thing about living in a castle was that it was a whole lot better than sleeping under a hedge.

Stefan Stinkle made his way down the steep stone stairs. He hated walking down the steps at night. They were worn down by hundreds of feet, and he found it hard to keep his balance in the dark. There were no electric lights, only a few candles on the walls. Freezing gusts of wind whistled around his ears. The flickering flames made shadows jump and twist on the walls.

Stefan shivered. Who could know what was waiting around the next curve? Or what was creeping down the stairs behind him? Anything could be following him in the shadows. He would never know until it was too late.

When Stefan reached the warm, noisy kitchens, he felt much better. The kitchens were filled with the steamy smells of food and the loud chatter of the servants. The cook was a huge man with hands like shovels. He was always dressed in a greasy robe and Stefan was usually scared of him. But tonight he looked normal and human.

"What do you want, young Stinkle?" he roared.

"Old Duncan sent me down to fill his goblet," said Stefan. "He's telling us a story."

"Dragons again, I suppose," the cook laughed, stirring a big saucepan full of soup. "He never talks about anything else."

Stefan filled the goblet and turned towards the stairs, wishing he could stay in the warm kitchens.

It was even worse going up than it had been coming down. The goblet was heavier, and Stefan puffed and panted as he climbed the steps. His breathing sounded very loud in his ears. Once again he began to have strange fears. Was that a sound, lower than the howling of the wind? Was that someone else breathing, louder than his ragged breaths? Was something waiting for him just above in the darkness? Surely there had been more light on the way down? By the time Stefan reached the open doorway of the Great Hall, he was in a real panic. His mouth felt dry and his legs trembled.

Stefan could see the flickering orange light from the fire through the doorway. He had never wanted to see the rest of the lads so much before. But as soon as he stepped inside the room, he knew that something was wrong. Very wrong. Terrifyingly wrong.

The Great Hall was much smokier than Stefan had remembered. Thick clouds of warm, white smoke billowed across the floor. The smoke started winding itself around Stefan's legs and swirling up towards his face.

Stefan was sure the room had not been as hot as this before. After the cold stairway, the Great Hall seemed too warm and stuffy.

Stefan rubbed his eyes. He peered through the smoke at the fireplace. He could see only one figure, standing with its back towards him. There was no sign of the other lads he had left behind. There were no hunting dogs panting beside the fire. Stefan gave a cold shiver of fear. There was an odd silence in the room.

Then, from the fireplace, the figure spoke.

"Ah, Stefan Stinkle," he said in a deep, dreadful voice, "I wonder how much you have guessed of what has happened here today?"

Stefan knew the voice. It was Duncan Dobetter! He tried to answer, but he could not speak. He knew he should run away, but his legs felt as if they had been turned to stone. At last Stefan knew what had happened to Duncan Dobetter in the woods all those years ago.

"Well, Stefan, what *do* you know?" said Duncan, with a hint of impatience in his voice. "You see," he continued, "there are only three things that can happen if a human meets a dragon. The human may kill the dragon. The dragon may kill the human. Or…"

Stefan finally found his voice. "Or the human becomes a dragon," he whispered. "I didn't know…I mean I don't…I don't want to…"

"Don't you?" hissed Duncan. "Oh, I think you do, Stefan. As soon as I saw you, I knew what a very fine dragon you would make. You with your jealousy of everyone else. You with your interest in fame and treasure. You with your cold, cold heart. Oh yes, you would make a truly splendid dragon. Will you really miss those other lads, do you think?"

"No," said Stefan Stinkle, and his cold heart became even colder.

"Welcome to the dragon world," said Duncan, and the smoke swirled up to hide the figure in the doorway.

Two minutes later, an old man and a boy left the Great Hall and walked down the stairs. They both looked ordinary enough – until their shadows flickered across the wall.